Brutal

Aiden Shaw was born in London in 1966. He attended youth theatre before going on to college, studying creative, then expressive arts. Aiden worked in the media, directing pop promos, taking photographs, acting and modelling. Whilst continuing his visual and performance art interests he made a living as a prostitute, also starring in hardcore pornographic films in California. Aiden is currently writing songs and performing with his band 'Whatever'.

Brutal

Aiden Shaw

Millivres Books
Brighton

Published in 1996 by Millivres Books (Publishers)
33 Bristol Gardens, Brighton BN2 5JR, East Sussex, England

Reprinted 1996

Brutal
Copyright © Aiden Shaw, 1996
The moral rights of the authors have been asserted

A CIP catalogue record for this book is available from the British Library

ISBN 1 873741 24 3

Typeset by Hailsham Typesetting Services, 4-5 Wentworth House,
George Street, Hailsham, East Sussex BN27 1AD

Printed and bound by Biddles Ltd, Woodbridge Park,
Guildford, Surrey GU1 1DA

Distributed in the United Kingdom and Western Europe by Turnaround
Distribution Co-Op Ltd., 27 Horsell Road, London N5 1XL

Distributed in the United States of America by InBook, 140 Commerce
Street, East Haven, Connecticut 06512, USA

Distributed in Australia by Stilone Pty Ltd, PO Box 155, Broadway, NSW
2007, Australia.

Thanks to all the people who have inspired this book, all the people who have supported me and all the people I love.

Mark Almond, Mark Beard, Scot Beveridge, Ray Brady, Simon Burt, Gorden Bowen, Ken Bunch, Peter Burton, Claire, Danny Cockerline, Devlane, Donald, B.J. a.k.a. Paul Goddard, Michael Fitzgerald, G, Richard Hindmarsh, David Hodgson, Joe Holtzman, Derek Jarman, Josie Jones, Kathleen, Paul Reeves, Johnny Poor Thing, Julian Thomas, Bruce Lahey, Mark Langthorne, Phillip, Josh Marcroft, Lawrence Malice, Paul Ruderford, Steve Maguire, Maire, Daniele Minns, Nancy, Sky, Trisha Stevens, 'S' and Peter, Marcus Wayland, Jess Wood, Sheila Roche, Paul Swainey and Gareth Owen.

Dedicated to David Michael.

CHAPTER ONE

I can't remember if the drugs were numbing my body, or if I was still too high to care. I was lying on a grimy lino floor, my face flattened with my mouth open wide. A puddle of what looked like murky saliva had cooled against my lips, yet my mouth was dry and tasted of something. I had been sick but because I hadn't eaten for three days all I could muster from my stomach was a cocktail of vodka and bile. I stood, although I felt as though I melted upwards. My brain was receiving distorted information from my senses and in turn it was sending out confused impulses for my motor skills. I could see it was daytime but hadn't the first idea as to what time it was or even which day it was.

Out of the window there was a London of run-down council flats that became obscured by a thick drizzling mist. Hanging out from the walls in the tiny room around me were syringes, many of them. They had been thrown like spears after use, to damage them. I didn't know where I was. I walked through a doorway keeping one hand against the wall for balance. I looked into the first room I came to. On a dressing table were some open jars, there were bags of clothes and a large smear of what looked like blood on one of the yellow walls. I carried on along the corridor and went in to another room which looked even less inviting but there was someone in a bed. I pulled back the cover and had to walk around the man to try and work out who it was. Some thoughts fitted together in a sloppy way to make a rough sketch of who I was with and where. Why I was there was much more complicated so left me confused. I felt a rip of disappointment and started to cry. I was scared. I tried to wake up the man but he was lifeless. I desperately needed some comfort. I got into the bed next to the stranger. I didn't want to cuddle him but did anyway. It was as though by going through the motions of affection it might really create the feeling and I might receive some warmth. But I didn't really know what I wanted. I gave up.

My body convulsed. I rolled over to avoid this happening again, as I did I saw some old feet with broken toes and cracked nails behind a pile of clothes. I tried to focus my attention on them but then realised that I was hallucinating. There was no way someone could fit behind such a small heap. I wanted to call someone, a friend, but I didn't know how to do this. I lifted my hand to wipe my eyes. Sitting on top of my main vein was a tiny bloody hole. Where the red dried and smeared away, the pink of an infection took over and covered an area about the size of my hand. I prodded the sore and a weird sensation ran up my neck. It was not my imagination this time. I passed out.

I had gone out on the Thursday night to a club and when I finally collapsed it was sometime early in the morning on the following Tuesday.

I looked up at my therapist and couldn't help laughing. This I explained, was why I had missed my last session with her and had not kept my appointments all the other weeks before that. I had been referred for treatment by my G.P. about two months previously and had got around to going three times up to that day.

Gary was the man in the bed that Tuesday morning, I was seeing a lot of him at that time. He was a drug dealer, so always had plenty of whatever I wanted, so I always had plenty of time for him. The sex I had with him was always intense which I loved when I was high. Of course it was probably only because I was high. There were times when we were so high that we couldn't even manage to have sex.

Gaia, my psychotherapist, listened very well and made me feel as though she liked me. She was paid to make me feel comfortable, but I could never help thinking that she did like me, at least a little. I had to believe this or I wouldn't have been able to carry on seeing her. The first thing I thought when I heard her name was, I like that. The second was, I wonder why her parents called her that? The third was, I wonder if it really is her name and if it is, it's so funny. These were all before I found out that it was the name of the Greek goddess of the earth, 'Earth Mother'. From then on I decided that it must be real because it

2

couldn't be a name one would choose oneself, especially for a therapist, it would be too silly and pretentious. I wondered what her parents might have possibly wanted from a child called Gaia. What were they saying about their own disappointments and dreams in life? As with every question I asked Gaia, her answer was to look at the question for the intention behind it. So when I asked her about her name, she smiled and almost laughed, then suggested that I might want to learn more about her as I might want to learn more about my mother. Her suggestions weren't always so tedious and obvious but I didn't know that then and thought, oh dear what am I doing here. I had already read about these theories at sixteen and seventeen when trying to work out my teenage problems.

When I asked about the way she dressed, I got a similar reply. I had to create the whole story as far as what I thought Gaia was and where she had come from. She wouldn't give me anything, saying,

'As long as I'm a mystery, you can't make me into anything in particular.'

I thought life was all about demystifying everything that I came across. Gaia knew better. I found I had nothing to grasp hold of, so I had nothing to hate, or pick holes in. I didn't know how educated she was. I didn't know her social class, or her sexuality, or in what part of the country she was born, or who she did or didn't like, nothing that I could judge her by. Nothing that I could destroy her with because I knew better. Gaia had hennaed hair. She wore familiar things. She didn't dress up or down, neither scruffy or prim. Her make-up was barely noticeable and she didn't wear perfume. I got what I could from all this, but decided that it wasn't enough not to be able to question any conclusion I came to.

Gaia's lack of being tended to help us focus on me. My insecurities had to be handled with great care. There were so many subjects that had to be covered on my Friday afternoon sessions in Ladbroke Grove. I would break down often, in those early days. As if she were a witch, all she had

3

to do was speak her incantations and she would reduce me to a mess of tears.

That morning as I left Gaia I was sweating, with my eyes still wet and my jaw taught. I was shivering. I tried to whistle but it sounded too wobbly. I tried to sing but couldn't control my breathing. It was no use, I was at the will of my body, which was at the will of my mind. I just don't know what the 'I' was then and how it all fitted together. Walking and trembling I arrived at The Lighthouse. As I sat in the dining room I gradually became less anxious. It was to become a regular thing, to have lunch in the café there on Fridays. Friends knew I would be there and would often arrange to meet me or sometimes just turn up. This was to become a nice thing for me, to have something regular that wasn't drug oriented.

The Lighthouse is a centre for people affected by HIV. There would often be sick people eating at tables or sitting in the garden, which I think was designed to be tranquil and beautiful. I tried to respect the intention and got what I could from it. There was always an air of something, or rather lots of things. It was a very special place, lots of people had spent their last days there and lots of friends had had to walk out from it to carry on their lives unhappy or relieved. I carried my own world into all the confusion, never unaware but always distracted.

I sat alone waiting for a friend who was already forty-five minutes late. My arm was itching from the infection. It reminded me to take the antibiotics that I had brought with me. The food in the café seemed designed to be easy to eat, high in fat, and both sweet and salty. I didn't feel like eating so got another cup of coffee. My palms were sweating so much that I had to keep wiping them on my jeans which had darker blue areas where I did this. I had a bad headache so asked the man behind the till if there were any pain killers in the kitchen that I could have.

The till-man got used to me coming in and as he did his attitude towards me seemed to change from friendly to lecherous. Where he had once greeted me with 'Hello,' this had changed to 'Hello, sex-pot'. I'm sure it was meant with

4

affection but when coming straight from therapy these tiny affirmations pierced my skin with a rush of response that didn't feel healthy.

"How many would you like?"

"How many does it say I should take?"

"One or two tablets . . . Every four hours, but no more . . ."

I waited until he finished his little song and dance.

"Three please." I smiled to counterbalance my paranoia about sounding strained. Then feeling self-conscious I explained. "I've got a bad headache." This was something I was used to. My head ached nearly every day, so I generally took a lot of pain killers.

I would have left but didn't want to face the street again just yet, then luckily Marcus came in. I had met this young man nearly seven years before. I was in London for the weekend, having travelled up from Brighton where I was in my second year of art college. It was a Sunday night and I knew that if I wanted to get the train back the next morning I had to be up early. I decided to go a small club which wasn't central but was near where I was staying. I got my drink and pretended to read the papers whilst standing in a good spot for all round viewing. It hadn't been an interesting weekend so far and I was quite bored. I wanted sex, but more than this I wanted some fun. I had a few beers, each with a vodka chaser. I went next door to where the dance floor was having waited until I thought it might have 'hotted up'. It was full and dark. All of the people seemed to merge into one as though they were simply a crowd. I walked through them towards the flashing lights which were absorbed by the muddy movements of the people. As I got through, a twirling head caught the light then dodged out of sight. When finding my space I watched as a young boy spun with his hands beside his face, so pretty and completely mad looking. He tossed and posed, kicked and shone amid a sea of darkness. He saw me as soon as I stood still and seemed to play up even more as though there was no one else around him although I thought he must be doing it for them, or rather against them. Whatever, it looked beautiful. He was

5

beautiful, but a real beautiful, which did not intimidate but drew me in. This may have been because it wasn't sexual or that it was before I was bothered by such things. Maybe it was as simple as I was attracted to him and went with it. I wanted fun but couldn't compete with this star so caught him as he came off. This wasn't difficult because he happened to come off right beside me as though there was no other space in the whole club.

"Excuse me," he said and kind of fell into me.

I got hold of him by his arm half helping him but pulling him towards me so that he had to look at me to see what was going on.

"You're a beauty," I said close in his ear.

He stopped as though timing his response to the second, then kissed me on my lips. Off he shot towards the bar and then suddenly was with me again with two drinks in his hand.

Marcus came home with me that night. We didn't have sex but I don't think it was for the more complex reasons that developed later in my life. Marcus swears that I said he was too beautiful to have sex with. Although that's exactly the kind of explanation he would give. All I know now is that I wanted him around and it turned out that so did lots of other people. Marcus was very popular and seemed to know everybody in London. I lured him home with the possibility of having sex. This was one of the ways in which I attracted people. Some say this is manipulating but if the goal is friendship how wrong is it?

When we woke up we decided to have breakfast with the drag queen I was staying with. I planned to go into college late, as I often did but sometimes I would end up staying in London the whole week. Before we left the house, Marcus picked up a lipstick and applied it as though it were the most usual thing to do on a Monday morning. It looked so odd on him for he had no other make-up on, just a boyish angelic face, the blondest hair, pink cheeks and ears then a bright red mouth that seemed to cover the whole bottom half of his face.

This was the Marcus I had grown to love, so was glad

6

that he did eventually turn up at The Lighthouse that day. He was very twitched and I could see that he was still high. He sat down, told me that he hadn't slept and wanted to go for a drink. This sounded like a good idea to me or at least an idea that meant I wouldn't have to be alone. We started on straight vodka and another weekend began.

CHAPTER TWO

We left The Lighthouse and were going from bar to bar getting more and more drunk until we realised we were getting sloppy. By mistake I knocked over someone's drink. We had to take some speed to level us out, otherwise we would have crashed out. We went to the toilet, cleaned off the cistern with a piece of tissue and made two big lines. Within fifteen minutes our heads seemed clear again, we felt chatty and funny with lots of energy. Marcus dragged me round to a club which was straight on Fridays but had a gay night on Wednesday so I had been to it before but really couldn't see the point of going on that day. Marcus said that he wanted to introduce me to a girlfriend of his who worked on the door. He had spoken of her before and I did think she sounded fun. When we got to the front of the club all I could see were bouncers. Then I heard a squeal and the mob of bouncers peeled open to reveal a woman.

"You must be Paul," she said and smiled.

"Hello, you must be Josie." Her face shone like I wish mine would. I warmed to her immediately, it seemed as though I had no choice. The bouncers snorted and shuffled their feet. We were making too much noise.

"They're with me," she said showing us in. Within seconds Josie and I were laughing and playing. We weren't allowed much time as Marcus had a list of places to fit in that evening. The deed had been done, he was very generous with his friends and his time and his money. I was very grateful to him for introducing me to Josie. I managed to see her again soon, by getting Marcus to take me with him when he went to meet her next. It wasn't long before I had her telephone number and used it. When calling she would always let the answer machine pick up the call so she could hear who it was. There was often a fraction of a second in those early days when I would imagine her sitting around with friends and laughing and wishing that she hadn't given me her number.

One night about two weeks later I was with a group of friends and we decided to carry on partying after the regular night-club had finished. There was only one place open. We all jumped in a cab and were working the nerves of the people on the door within minutes. There was a problem. No women were allowed in on Thursdays, it was strictly men only. A sexy/cruise crowd is how it was described on the flyer. No Josie. I think it was because she felt it her fault that we didn't get in, that she invited us all back to her place. Firstly I went down stairs to pick up some ecstasy, then we all headed to Josie's flat in South Kensington. It was good to feel like she wanted me in her home and that she accepted the friends I had with me. I felt that she was so special and she made me feel like I had worth. If I was to say now what I wanted from Josie it would seem so far from what I was getting but firstly I didn't know then what I wanted and secondly I felt grateful for something already. I know now that I wasn't capable of accepting then what she eventual did offer me.

These weeks rolled by in a continual blur and I still don't understand what I was doing, what was going on in my head. Gaia has suggested that I was abusing myself but I thought that I was looking for fun. I realised it was an extreme way of treating myself but I managed to justify it on an intellectual level. I felt I was learning by stretching myself. How far can I go? What will happen if I do this? then this? and what if? I knew it was hard on my body and my mind but I considered myself hard.

I found myself in Trade most Saturday nights. This club attracted an extreme crowd, very drug oriented, very gay with lots of transvestites, sex changes and plain old drag. Although everyone was high it was always very serious. The dancing was serious. The sexual to and fro was intense. There was one sex change called Lola who was well known for fucking under the stairs, near the dance-floor, with her straight boyfriend. Sex in the toilets was common, along with people taking drugs. There were some who would use them because they had the shits from their E or others who just stood or sat staring, thinking that any second some piss would come out. It didn't really matter how long they took as everyone in the queue would lose track of time. Cocaine and speed had to be taken in the toilet because they didn't usually come in the more convenient tablet form like ecstasy.

Trade ended on Sunday afternoon and the crowd usually went straight over to the next club, which went on all day to link up with a Sunday all nighter called ff back in the same place where Saturday night had been spent. It always looked as though nobody had left. There was a rumour one week that someone had been found on Monday afternoon dead under the stairs and that they had been there since Saturday. Marcus joked that surely Lola would have noticed if this were true. No one knew the person so it passed over.

Everybody knew that either of these places were difficult to handle unless you were very high, not just high. What I would generally do is start off by getting drunk then take some E to make me feel more friendly, then some speed to keep me awake and help me dance. Of course, if anyone had coke that would help with confidence and again clear the head a little. Alcohol would be a continual downer in case I found myself getting too high, which was usual. I always carried a few prescription Valium or Rohypnol for emergencies and in case I ended up somewhere and didn't want to be awake anymore. This only occurred if I left my friends to go and have sex and then my partner fell asleep or if I began to ache from being up too long and had to sleep from complete exhaustion. This aching wasn't a muscular ache it was as though everything in my body was saying enough, my organs, my skin, my teeth and my joints, everything. This is when convulsions began and I tended to hallucinate even if I hadn't taken acid. I just wouldn't be able to function properly anymore. It was painful to be awake so I would take another drug to stop it all.

I was at this stage one particular weekend but took the other cure all option. I left the club and went to a friends house nearby to IV some speed. This was always a great trick on Sunday mornings, the last two or three days of lack of sleep and lots of vodka would just dissolve. The speed warmed my blood with that familiar squirting sensation, then a healthy glow flushed to my cheeks and with a quick giggle I went back to the club. Of course when more organised I would prepare a couple of needles beforehand, using coke or speed or even ecstasy. I would tuck them down my sock to use in the toilets.

One particular weekend I had just rejuvenated myself in this way and talked my way down two flights of stairs. Settling myself in a comfortable corner under a bright light I entertained myself. I knew I could take on any body at that moment or any situation especially as I knew everyone else in the club was beginning to fade.

From a quick scan of the sweaty room I caught sight of what looked like Josie's pale skin turning at the entrance. My instant reaction was to shout her name loudly so that everyone in the room turned round and sure enough so did she. That smile was there again. She dropped her company and came walking across. I couldn't have given her a warmer welcome. For me it were as though something real had finally just happened in all the madness. Through the coating of drugs it took just a smile and then there was something more. Josie and I sat together for the rest of that night and seemed to retract from the action until we had our legs closed, knees together and were bent over being very private. A girl approached us, she seemed unaware of personal space and whatever etiquette we had jut created for ourselves. She was wearing a bra, hot-pants and along with her hair they were soaked with sweat.

"Hi, I'm Sara. Got any gum?" Josie shook her head.

"Have you?"

"No sorry."

"Got any water?" She said to Josie.

"No sorry only vodka."

"Ugh, I don't know how you can drink that stuff." Sara carried on talking at Josie who smiled and put up with her. This gave me my first chance to have a good look at my new friend. She looked so out of place in Queer where all the boys, buff or frail were stripped down to their waists and most of the girls too. Josie was seemingly cool in an elegant long black dress that ended over a pair of Doctor

11

Marten boots. A thin coating of pale foundation and possibly some clear lip balm was all the make-up I could see on her face but her shiny hair was died black and hung very straight. She was back-lit by a burning candle which seemed to make her glow. I don't know if it was the drugs which emphasised this but the overall effect gave me a warm sensation in my gut. I looked back at Sara grinding her jaw and straightening her bra. Then I looked back at Josie who looked so delicate, yet I felt safe with her. Sara was gone in a moment, off in search of gum.

I began to tell Josie about a friend of mine. I would not ordinarily mention her to most, she was a different part of my life that I knew I had grown away from and I felt very sad that this had happened. I wanted to share this with Josie and could only intimate what it was. I don't think she understood what I was trying to explain, but I got the feeling she realised that there was someone else who related to me on a different level or about different things than what was around us in Queer. This other woman's name was Loz.

I looked around the room and caught the eye of a Brazilian boy who was sitting at the top of a pyramid of boys draped across a table and chairs. The furniture couldn't be seen, only the bodies stripped down to their waists, sweating, all silent and dazed. It was early in the morning and who was going to go home with whom must have been one of the main thoughts going through most of their minds.

I had fucked in the toilet earlier with a boy who had given me lots of drugs. As always it was hazy as to whether I wanted the drugs or the dick, either way I had had enough sex for now. The boy across from me untangled himself and came across. I knew he was coming but carried on my slow conversation with Josie, maybe he would be distracted on the way across, or change his mind and go and dance.

"Paul, I didn't realise that was you here all this time. I was thinking who's that hot boy over there with that beautiful girl?" Jose-Antonio was a charmer and he knew I liked him for this. Josie smiled at him. I couldn't help smiling also. At that time of the morning a compliment was always welcome whether drug induced or not. I knew that he meant it to a certain extent because we had sex without drugs quite a few times and he had seemed sincere then. The trouble was that there was another idea wavering in my mind. It was nearly closing time and he wanted sex and I was quite sure he didn't care too much with whom. We chatted briefly and I said I would come and say good-bye before I left which gave us both the option of possibly going home together, but without committing ourselves. I knew I would be comfortable with Jose-Antonio even though I knew it was not what I was really looking for.

I wasn't sure yet whether Josie would be the right choice to come down off drugs with either. I turned back to her and we both acknowledged the situation. Josie had been around gay men long enough to know that I would probably end up with Jose-Antonio. "He looks lovely. You should go home with him, there's no point in wasting your high."

At that moment Josie had shown to me that she understood how I felt, but more than that, she understood my depths. Of course I was lonely and of course an outsider could have seen that Josie might offer me what I needed more so than this boy. I needed affection badly, so from inside it felt like I had no choice. This encounter seemed superficial but as was so often the case I dealt with my depths in a superficial way.

The term 'depths' used in this way was something I had borrowed from Loz and like so many things in life once you learn the language for your thoughts it can help you understand the meaning of things you feel. I found this to be true. It was why I liked to talk to people to see if they had finished ideas that I might have still been working on. Sometimes older people had but equally there were those who just seem to have insight for no apparent reason. I could feel that there was a connection between Josie and Loz which I wanted to keep hold of. Loz was quite inaccessible, I could speak to her on the phone but I rarely went to visit her yet it was during visits or when she wrote to me that ground was covered and depths were reached. Josie was at hand, I was glad of this.

13

At Jose-Antonio's we had wild sex which seemed to go on for ever. When we got back to his place we took some acid which slows sex down and tends to make it very sensual. I don't know if I slept but eventually it was time for me to leave. It was Sunday afternoon and I was going to head home but decided instead to go by a bar called The Covent Garden Tavern. It was a leather/denim bar which was busy on Sundays because it was one of the few bars open all day. When I got there I was immediately given some more acid by a friend. By Sunday afternoon it was sometimes the easiest drug to get hold of for free because it was so cheap and so strong nobody ever minded sharing their tab. I was bought a few drinks by some people that I used to hang out with but hadn't seen for ages.

One weekend, several years earlier, when I had been helping them sell stuff, we had been busted by the drug squad. Two of them had been sent down but were now free again. Luckily I had got off completely but this scared me enough not to be so blatant about my dealings after that.

I kept on drinking and was given some more acid and then some more. Technically you can't overdose on acid but I ended up lying on the grass outside this bar and retching. I could no longer walk or see properly. I could barely talk. My friends thought this was funny and rolled around beside me laughing. A stranger came to me and I remember him checking my pulse for some reason and asking me was I okay. I managed to ask him to get an ambulance. I wouldn't have done this unless I thought it was really necessary. Soon after it arrived, I was taken to Charing Cross Hospital. There was no point in pumping my stomach because the acid was already in my blood stream so a nurse was assigned to stay beside me to make sure I didn't choke as I vomited.

Nothing made any sense to me and everything I could see seemed to break apart and the pieces scatter. I wailed continually, clinging on to the nurse's hand. I was terrified. It took about eleven hours of living hell before I could function again properly. I was asked questions to check I had my head together. I felt so fragile. One of the nurses

14

gave me the money to get a cab home, he was so kind. I was shaken by the whole of this experience for some time so never felt like taking acid after that. I remember being annoyed that I had missed ff.

My birthday fell on a bank holiday about a month later. After Queer Marcus and I had gone with some boys who lived together in a house in Russell Square. Sunday we partied all day, with different people popping in and out. I had plenty of coke so we could carry on endlessly. At the time I used to sell small amounts of coke. I had about six regular buyers. I would buy an ounce or two, split it and sell it in grams. I never cheated them, just sold it at the going rate which always left a couple of grams for me in profit. Everyone was happy. My dealer trusted me. He made a profit and I got wasted. The thing was when you have a regular supply like this other things come your way easily. For example, one weekend someone might be low and I might offer them some coke just when they really needed it and then they're a friend for life. Then when they have excess they sort you out. This kind of bartering went on continually and sometimes sex became involved because drugs could always be used as incentive for someone else to come home with you or you to go home with them.

The next day, Monday morning, my supply of coke had run out. We had already moved on to cheap speed and vodka to get us through and by lunch time we were very speedy, very drunk and feeling pretty rancid. We decided to go back to my place because the hosts of the never ending party were obviously getting bored with us. I was with two other people as well as Marcus and although I had only met them that Saturday at Trade we all wanted to stick together. We had been together in one room talking nonsense and acting stupid for over twenty four hours, in which time we had grown accustomed to each other. Often on drugs this bonding takes place with strangers, this is especially noticeable on ecstasy. It feels as though you understand everybody, where they're coming from and why they're behaving the way they are. It can get to the point where you can feel spiritually connected with others for no reason and believe it wholeheartedly. In this state we all arrived back at my house as the telephone rang.

"Hello."

"Hello is that Brad?"

"Yeah, that's right."

"Is it possible to come and see you?"

"Have I seen you before?"

"No, I got your number from one of the papers."

I had used the name Brad to advertise on-and-off for years now.

"When were you thinking of?"

"Now if possible." I covered the mouthpiece.

"It's a punter. I can't do him now, I feel wretched."

At this Marcus grinned. "What are you thinking?"

"Oh just a idea."

"What?"

"We could get some more stuff."

"How? We've got no money left."

"We can pay for it tomorrow with the money you earn."

"Genius."

There was someone he could get it from within two minutes walk. The plan was to run, pick up the stuff and free-base it before the customer got round.

"Could you make it in an hour's time?"

"Yes, that would be fine." I gave him the address and everything went smoothly. The idea was that we had the coke and before we could actually come down we would take some Rohypnol and drift off painlessly. I even enjoyed doing the customer although I can't remember what he looked like or what we did.

CHAPTER THREE

There was a change as to which sleeping tablets could be prescribed on the national health. I would have to see the resident psychologist at Chelsea and Westminster to get the ones I wanted. I had to be assessed to make sure that I really needed them. So the appointment was made and the day came. I was walking by the main entrance on my way to the mental health department and I heard someone call my name.

I turned round to see Kevin. If I had loved anyone in my life up to that point, it would probably have been this man. I was eighteen when I met him. I thought of him as an older man although he was only twenty-six. Kevin had me to mould. I was at a stage in my life where he could have made anything of me. I believed in him. When he told me I was clever or creative I felt so strong. He told me I could succeed at whatever I wanted. The trouble was this also had a negative side and when he told me I was shit, which he did, or when he rejected me, which he did, I was left feeling pathetic and lame. This happened quite definitely one day. I had hitch-hiked about two hundred miles to see him. We were living in different cities whilst I was meant to be deciding whether or not I should move. I was going to surprise him and had planned to just turn up. When I arrived he boldly introduced me to his new boyfriend who was taking a bath. I was asked to shake hands with a beautiful naked man sitting in the water smiling. I remember thinking how happy he looked in his new flat, with his new boyfriend, in a new and exciting country. This new man was American and looked like everything I could ever have dreamt of wanting. I couldn't feel anger towards him or jealousy. He simply overwhelmed me. I think at that point, standing in that claustrophobic little bathroom, I felt uglier than I had ever felt in my life and so awkward. I didn't dare show any emotion or I might have realised how ridiculous I really was. They sat and talked whilst I was left sitting in the living room. Kevin eventually came through and said that I could spend the night if I wanted and that it was okay by them. I left.

Here was that man in front of me, who had had me to mould, who himself had been defeated and wizened with his life force seemingly sucked from him.

"Paul. I'm just getting out of here." His head gestured towards the C&W.

"How are you?" It hit me instantly what was probably wrong with him and he seemed to want to tell me. I was getting more used to this kind of conversation, so let him lead.

"I've got cancer. It's my bone marrow."

I'm the kind of person who doesn't even like to think we are made up of things like bone-marrow let alone that it can get diseased.

"Is it HIV related?"

"Yes, but the chemo seems to have been really successful." As he carried on talking it struck me how I was reacting, managing to converse, showing little emotion. "I've got to slow down and try to adjust to all this. I'm going to Thailand. I've never been. I should be able to survive okay on my sickness benefit. I'll see."

"Kevin. There's something I want to talk to you about." I looked at the woman beside him, having barely registered her until now.

"Oh sorry, this is my social worker, Cathy."

"Hello, Cathy." I had to carry on despite her being there. "Kevin . . . I can't forgive you for the way you treated me." He laughed in the way that he always had, making me feel stupid.

"Let's talk," he said.

He still affected me so much.

"I'll call you. I'm late. I'm seeing the psychologist here."

"Call soon, because I'll be going away, to Thailand." It seemed as though by reaffirming this, it might really make it happen.

"I'd love to. Bye, Cathy, nice to meet you. Bye, Kevin, look after yourself. I'll call you at the end of the week."

I ran round the corner feeling nervous. My doctor took some time to see me and when she finally did I told her what had just happened. I cried for about twenty minutes as

18

I tried to answer her questions. She told me as I left that I would most likely be able to get the tablets I wanted but my psychotherapist would have to be contacted first.

I called Kevin every other day after that but couldn't get a reply. Selfish bastard, I thought, he probably left for Thailand without thinking twice about our conversation. I saw the boyfriend from the bathtub, they had finished years ago but I knew they still saw a lot of each other.

"Tell Kevin, thanks for calling back." From the response on his face I knew I had just got it really wrong.

"Paul, Kevin died last Thursday. I tried to get hold of you." So many ideas flashed through my mind, angry, self pitying, vulnerable thoughts and such sadness.

I never liked crying in front of people, but Gaia had created a space for me to do this, so as I recalled the incident to her she passed me tissue after tissue. These all got very wet because my hands were sweating as well.

"I stood listening to Kevin whilst he told me that he was dying and I felt nothing."

Gaia had become for me, not essential, but one of the most interesting and interested people I spoke to at that time.

"You're not feeling nothing now though, are you?"

"No, I guess not."

"I would suggest that you didn't feel 'nothing' when you spoke to Kevin. I think maybe you pretend to yourself that things like this have no impact. I suggest we try and look at how things do affect you and to what degree. I think its kind to allow ourselves a reaction." I stopped crying and looked at her. "If someone cuts you do you bleed?" I nodded. I felt foolish, as though I had believed I was invincible, foolish and possibly vain but with my eyes now a little more open. This was to become an important part of what I learnt from Gaia. What impact things had on me and what impact I had on others. This crossed many areas of my life from how what I say affects my mother to how I may be affected by the way my customers treat me. Maybe more obvious to others was the idea that the chemicals I put in my brain and the ways I let other men relate to me sexually; in fact I was unaware of the impact most things had in my life.

19

As I left Gaia I almost bumped into Josie on the street. She was on her way to meet me. We hugged.

"Your back's all wet." She looked concerned, but she meant it.

"I've just been sweating that's all." Josie looked into my eyes and could see that I had been crying. She just squeezed me again and held me just a little bit longer than usual. We linked up as we walked towards The Lighthouse. As we ate our lunch I noticed that there was a memorial on. It was someone else I knew, but not very well. I made a half-hearted attempt at indifference, then checked myself, remembering what Gaia had said about impact.

Kevin's memorial was held about a week later. I went by myself for there was no one currently in my life who knew him. I recognised faces from the past, people I remembered not liking. The service was a series of events. The coffin brought in. The coffin laid on an altar. The artificial rolling motion. The velvet looking curtains lifting and then closing. All of a sudden it was over. He had gone trundling on into the crematorium. I almost missed his get away. I was too busy wondering what I was thinking about, which happened to be how kooky this all was. As I watched the tassels gently swishing I began to feel annoyed. Couldn't there have been a better warning or something to add emphasis to the last seconds this body would be on the planet. I couldn't help thinking how pathetic Kevin was. It seemed so apt that he would go like this, not making it nice for me, not bothered what the show was like. Then the horrid woman who had led the service wanted to shake my hand on the way out. I wanted to spit at her but I reluctantly did what I was supposed to do, in submission or rather confusion.

This carried over to my next session with Gaia. It took some time for me to admit that I felt angry but she got it out of me.

"I think maybe you're confusing this anger," she explained. As usual I sat there, desperate for her words, trying to fit everything in order. "I would suggest that you were probably angry at the service, the way Kevin was dealt with, how pathetic it made him seem." Gaia was using my words but putting them together in a way that made more sense. "Not in fact angry at him at all. Maybe we should look at these things separately."

"Why am I so angry at the way he was treated? He's dead now. What does it matter?"

"I would like to ask why you might have been so confused about this to begin with?"

Gaia was going straight to the underlying point here.

Up until now I had professed to not care so much for Kevin. I would not give that to him, not after what he did to me.

"I think maybe you cared for Kevin more than you admit." She must have known this the moment I spoke about Kevin and, as she had a habit of doing, she hit me in the face with it, making me feel as stupid as any school teacher ever had. I loved Kevin, these words span through my mind and burst out in the form of tears. Gaia makes it all seem so simple although it's generally a tough journey getting there. No matter how stupid she makes me feel or how sad, it's always within the confines of therapy. A safe environment had been created for all my shit to be dealt with. It was at times a cruel awakening and at times a home-coming. Ideas would come into my head that she had fed me at their last stage of development. I would often be allowed to do the final shaping, then out would come discoveries. It seemed like I knew the answers all the time. I say seemed because Gaia was actually constructing the whole thing. That isn't to say that it was not real. I see it now as though I had crumbled and at times shattered and Gaia was simply saying: here you forgot to pick up this piece of puzzle. I, the child, would take it and thank her.

I walked out from my session that day with the new found idea that I might have truly loved Kevin. This meant a lot to me as, I'm sure, Gaia intended. A seed had been sown in that last hour. A seed that held the beginnings of a life, a life in which I was capable of love and if that was true it might be possible again. I set to work in my mind trying to decipher the good feelings I had felt for Kevin. It was early days yet though. I still hated him.

21

CHAPTER FOUR

It had been in the last two years in particular that my drug taking had become the biggest part of my life, in fact it was all my life. Everything else had become mere inconveniences. Things that my life used to be about slipped into hazy memories, and that's what I thought them to be, somehow lost, reassured that my life had changed and I could do nothing about it. What I had become I had to accept, for I felt there was no way to change this new life. There was an element of doubt to this or perhaps hope. I knew from the past that I had managed to change things before. When I was twenty-one I was drinking heavily and taking a lot of downers. I would go home at night with some young man I had picked up and not even manage to have sex. When I woke up in the morning I generally would have no idea where I had been, what I had done, or who was lying next to me. Then one night as I staggered home I had a sudden realisation. I don't know if it was inspired by the fact that I was on my own and this was something I was certain I didn't want. I seemed to look at myself from a distance and what I saw was sad. I saw a boy not a man who was making his experiences blurred. In those days I wasn't so deeply disturbed as I became later. Whether this was due to eventual greater drug abuse or prostitution or neither of these, who knows? My life then seemed simpler. I just lived.

I know for a fact that this isn't true, if I look at old diaries I find I was always torturing myself with the same ideas and even some others.

In this drunken sedation, how much was I missing? It's hard to know, for I really wasn't aware of what was on offer. Maybe I could have had the world or maybe just a part of my youth that I will never have again. To spend seconds in this way let alone years can be looked on with regret by the old or the sick, or rather anyone who isn't given the choice. I saw myself dragging a figure, lost by my softer self, along the street and knowing that I wanted a change. I had a conversation inside my head.

"I want a change. I want this to stop."

"What do you want?"

"I want to stop drinking and taking drugs." Although these words were silent my face responded to everything I said. A grotesque and silent conversation was deciding my fate.

"Why don't you stop?"

"Because I can't."

"Do you mean that?"

"Yes."

"Are you sure this is true?"

"Yes, I'm sure of it."

"Is there any point of living then because you don't like what you are and you can't do anything about it. You may as well kill yourself."

"No . . . I don't want to."

"Then you could try and make a change. If you fail you will have lost nothing."

The conversation ended here. I realised that if I couldn't change I really wasn't worthy of my life. The next morning I started to make a change and I managed it for a while. Then along came ecstasy, which seemed harmless enough. Although once high it was generally a case of taking anything I could get my hands on. This compulsion was followed by desperation and an eventual neglect for anything outside my immediate needs. Relationships I had built became shadows where only gestures manage to hold them together. I could no longer put energy into them so people I knew had to be satisfied with an occasional "I love you". I hoped that it would suffice for I had forgotten what relationships were really meant to be about, like the time that has to be put in, being there for people, giving and accepting advice and opinions. I think perhaps deep down I knew that this was happening but wouldn't admit it to myself. This was a part of my sadness. I was missing out on the warmth of love. Again there was a coating over my eyes, a coating over my heart and an obstacle between different parts of myself. I know now that I'm too selfish to miss out for too long without wanting change but there

23

was a fear that I could equally be consumed by bitterness.

This time round everything was much more difficult. I suffered for my constant drug taking. I had mood swings, nervousness and panic attacks brought on by extreme anxiety. My paranoia verged on psychosis so I was unsure as to what was real. Together with all of this I felt anger and frustration at the thought that this was what I'd become.

There wasn't a single conversation this time, no sudden realisation, just an aggravating hum of discontent and misery. Everyone around me knew things had to change. They were patient and supportive and tried to allow me to do as I pleased. Then when they felt they could, they told me they were scared for me. I thought that I was special, that they hadn't gone so far because they didn't dare. They were terrified of stretching life to see what was really out there and more importantly deep inside. What they probably thought was that they didn't stretch it because they didn't want to. Perhaps that was not surprising if I was the example. Some would say that I wasn't even stretching it, I was just confusing it. As long as it was confused enough then I was safe in not having to deal with it.

CHAPTER FIVE

I had just finished wanking, out of boredom rather than frustration, when the telephone rang. I stood up and shuffled towards it with my trousers still round my ankles and my belt jangling on the floor. Cum dribbled down my stomach and onto my groin. I cupped it with one hand whilst picking up the receiver with the other equally slimy hand.

"Hi. It's Marcus."

The phone slipped out of my hand and clanked to the ground. I picked it up again.

"Sorry Marcus. I've got come all over my hands."

"Oh are you working?"

"No, playing."

"Listen." Marcus's voice changed as he guarded the receiver with his hand for privacy. "I've just sold this bloke three grams of coke and he wants to have some fun."

"So?"

"So I naturally thought of you."

"What does he want? I've just cum. I'm not going to be up to much. What does he like?"

"I don't know. Besides cocaine? Hang on I'll ask him."

I could hear a television as Marcus began to speak to him. Then through the confusion of noise I heard a loud effeminate slur.

"Marcus, tell him it's just visual," the punter said.

"He says . . ."

"Yeah, I heard him."

"Hang on Paul." I could hear what sounded like stammering as the punter conveyed his fetish. "He says he wants you to wear some gear . . . Sorry Paul, hang on . . . Stan I can't tell what your saying." More slur. "Yeah, sure thing . . ."

"He sounds a bit of a mess, Marcus."

Marcus lowered his voice again.

"Yeah he is, but I think he's harmless. He's got leather gear. I told him you're good fun and you like your coke.

25

You will have some won't you?"

"Yeah sure," I thought, it can't be that bad, getting high and dressing up. "How much will he pay?"

"Hang on . . . Two-fifty."

"Great, just give me the address. Does he want to talk to me?"

"No, he trusts me." Marcus was the kind of dealer people liked, he was fair, usually on time, and could get along with anybody.

I got a cab round to find Marcus had already left. Stan answered the door in a tight jock-strap which cut into his flat bum as he staggered up the stairs in front of me. He wasn't your average punter. He was younger, camp and cloney. He explained that he'd got sick of the scene and never got what he wanted.

The design of this flat was precise, with copies of screen prints on the walls of elegant women all in black and white except for bright red lips and nails. There was a clutter of gold ceramic figures on clear plastic podiums, a man's torso, a greyhound and a pair of hands. I was shown around as he tripped and stumbled. I think he was very drunk as well as high. I was shown his bed complete with a sling hanging from the ceiling. Also his kitchen with a huge notice board covered in pictures of actresses from the fifties, porn stars, and Polaroids of men who I guessed were previous trade. I was shown his bathroom in which the wall tiles, carpet, towels and soap were all black.

"Check out the ceiling, it's really sexy," he said with a lazy gesture whilst falling against the door frame. Above me I could see my reflection. I smiled at myself. I could see his hand holding his glass just behind my back.

"We'll get in there later . . ." he said, pointing at the red marbled bath. ". . .and I'll soap you up."

I shuddered at the thought.

"That'll be great," I said, thinking he probably wouldn't make it past the next half hour. I was offered some coke which I snorted. It was like oxygen to me. I had a whiskey, neat, it was the only alcohol he had. Soon I was getting messy too and it was time for the fun to begin. I was given a large black sports bag and was told to tip it out and pick out what ever I wanted to wear. Out poured the black gear which reminded me of the 'baddies' in fairy tales or the fantasies some people have about gay men and leather. I sifted through it.

"Shall I put these trousers on?"

"No, they're mine. Look the stripe's on the right side."

There was a yellow stripe all the way down the leg. I reminded myself that this was going to be just visual.

"I liked to be pissed on."

"Yeah, I guessed. Shall I put this on?"

"No, that's a passive harness."

"What would you like me to put on?" I said aggravated, whilst still trying to appear sexy and cool.

"Try that cock ring on." Big costume, I thought. "And leave your boots on."

I would have felt ridiculous if I wasn't so high. I tried to imagine what he was thinking, which I thought could have been: God he's crap at this, what a waste of money, or, Wow! what a sexy stud.

I was asked to walk around the room, to lean against walls, and to crouch down so my balls and dick hung between my legs.

"I like that," he said before he went down for another line, as though it was going to intensify his excitement or take the whole affair to a different realm, which no doubt it would do, at least in his mind, being even higher. There have been a few times when I've been sober in a crowd whilst they're high and really very little happens. Things are said that everyone else who's high seems to connect with, as though there is something more happening on another level and there is, it's simply the drug level.

Stan possibly believed he would release himself. Maybe he would just get more sloppy, more incoherent, more demanding, less respectful, and generally not give a damn if he did. It didn't really matter to me because I was off somewhere too. A part of me was getting into the posing and pretending to be hot; then another part of me was getting off on being able to think around what I was doing

27

and how it was all being affected by the drugs. My main concern became how I could consume as much of the coke on the table as possible. The whole event became a mess of him not being able to tell me what he wanted and me not being able to do what I thought he was trying to tell me to do. I think this went on for some time until I had the idea of getting us into the bedroom, presumably to get him to cum so that I could go.

My coked-up mind devised a plan as to what I wanted and looking back it seemed manipulative and selfish, so I shamelessly blame that on cocaine. I knew the punter wouldn't want to be left alone, so I had the idea of getting someone else to come round. At the time I knew two lovers who worked individually as prostitutes. I had a crush of lust for one of them and I got the impression the boyfriend inconveniently had one for me. I phoned them and asked if the one who liked me wanted to work. I explained that the money was good and that the customer was relatively easy.

"What you really want to do is get him to take a sleeping tablet. He's got Tamazipan beside his bed, and I know he has to get a flight tomorrow, so it shouldn't be too hard." After this briefing he decided he would come round. "Can I have a quick word with your boyfriend?" I added just before he put the phone down.

I explained that I was high and asked if I could go round. He said I could. All I can remember is fragments of the following hours. I left Stan's flat, borrowing a rubber mask. This mask looked like it could have been used in a horror film. It had press studs on it so that pieces could be attached to cover the mouth and eyes. It was actually a series of thick straps which buckled at the back. I left without getting paid. I was too high to care. I arrived at the boy's flat. I remember him asking me to wear the mask, then having my hands and feet winched up together with some clever and elaborate rope work. This was no beginner. The covering over my mouth would be removed now and then for his big cock to stuff through the barely big enough mouth piece. I was given poppers often and hardly knew whether I was up side down or inside out. I

28

knew that I wasn't aware of everything that was happening. I found this very satisfying as though I had been ripped free of this world and was floating in some heavenly unfeeling womb. I wanted the eye piece to be removed to see the monstrous thing that was attacking me. The beautiful face and body of the enemy, but I was not allowed that pleasure. I was made to suffer in blindness.

I went to bed late that night, wiped of inclination to do anything else. I slept a Rohypnol sleep and had nightmares I couldn't wake out of, no matter how hard I tried. In the morning I got up in a similar frame of mind as the one I'd gone to bed in. It hadn't been shaken off by sleep. I spent all day sitting and staring, getting up to make cups of tea, sitting down, then staring again. I thought about Marcus and Stan and the sex I had afterwards. I consciously tried to hold on to these thoughts to talk about the following day.

"When someone wants to be abused usually there is an abusive tendency also."

Gaia had mentioned this before but I hadn't really understood it fully. She had also suggested that within a relationship that involves abuse that the role is routinely swapped. One person may do something and the other feels wronged so reacts in an abusive way. "Look at it this way. When you fantasise, let's say when you masturbate, if you imagine yourself being abused where is that other character coming from? How is it formed? How do you know how to be that character?"

"Wow." I said. The idea never seemed clearer. Of course I had to be able to relate to the abuser or how could I recreate him.

I hadn't liked the idea that I could abuse. I hadn't thought I had this kind of anger within me. Gaia had brought it into my conscious thought.

CHAPTER SIX

At the beginning of another blurry week which followed an equally blurry weekend, I woke around three o'clock. I had lain in bed dreading the thought of having to start my day. I had to go to the toilet so eventually had to move. I noticed a letter at the front door and picking it up I recognised Loz's writing. The frank mark read Brighton, this was the confirmation. I also read the date and couldn't believe that four months had passed since Christmas. Loz lived on the coast with her girl friend Mary, who wasn't a girl at all, they were both in their mid-forties. These women's lives centred around their home, but they were far from insular. They had the ability, possibly because of their charisma and intelligence, to draw in life experiences from various sources. Perhaps it was just a craving for stimulation, but whatever it was, their enthusiasm seemed limitless. There were parts of their life that were obscured to me. I was only given shadowy sketches of their friends. I thought this might be because they thought I didn't have the patience for anything outside the here and now, the things at my arm's length. I think they may even have thought I'd be jealous. Their sex life was left a void to me and that was fine. These things did not seem to be a part of what they were to me.

Loz was a painter who had had a long education. Her first degree was in theology at Oxford her second in history of art at Sussex. Now she worked as a cleaner in the Brighton HIV and Aids drop in centre. Painting was her passion, although passion seemed the wrong word for it. Her way of working was slow, well thought out and well informed. I know this way of painting would be too tiresome or uninspired for a lot of artists but her way was to understand, interpret and express. It was because of her method that I felt I understood her work. It seemed to make sense to me that a painting be understood, that it had background and that communication was a part of the whole process. Her figures were characters, her landscapes

30

gave context and even her symbols gave extra clues.

I met Loz when I was nineteen, although she was introduced to me as Laura. A friend of mine from college arranged to meet her in a café one lunch break. From our first few words she managed to reach into me. I felt excited by her responses, she seemed to really listen, to really think and more unusually, to honestly tell me what it was that she was thinking. It would have been unnerving if I hadn't been so desperate for somebody that could communicate in this way. I felt exposed to her but like when I am with Gaia I felt that once she had opened me she would do no harm. Her intention seemed only to both nurture and learn more about me. I've learnt since then that she sees this as a role of hers. This is not an unthinking resignation, but a choice, knowing her strengths, willing to share them, to heal with them and even to love when needed. I needed. This was a slow process when dealing with me but she was persistent. The letter read

Dearest Paul,

In the depths, you and I are as one. I know you are on a journey down a road that I can't follow. Your voice shakes and your hands sweat. I am at the end of that road. Know that I will be waiting for you with my arms open. I will truly miss you until you arrive.

Love
Laura.

What was I to understand from this letter? I knew it needed no reply and I knew it was true. We were separated from where we were linked. What she spoke of is where I wanted to be. I didn't know how to get there but I knew I would be sad until I did.

Loz was religious but not in a way that was alienating for me. I had been brought up a Roman Catholic but didn't believe this was of any use to me anymore. When I first got to know her I had found her God hard to accept. Her use of

31

biblical figures and events seemed irrelevant to me. It took me around three years to understand that she was actually speaking in metaphors. Then as I understood what she meant by this, she took it a stage further.

"Why do you use metaphors? Why not just use plain language?"

"Well what is language, if not interpretation?"

I thought about this, it seemed straight forward enough. "It's as though you're trying to make something real out of something that doesn't exist."

"So don't you believe this stuff exists?"

"Well yes but not as stories. I understand it as emotion and thoughts."

"But that's why we use metaphors. It helps give shape to our inner-selves." Loz passed me a piece of home-made bread.

"But they're still only metaphors. Surely you don't really believe in all that religious kitsch?"

"Do you have to talk with your mouth full. Okay, the way I see it is, we happily believe that you can bend space time, or that everything is made of vibrating strings?"

"Yeah but that's science."

Loz makes a face imitating my stuffed cheeks. "Squirrel, you don't have to store it there's plenty more." I roll my eyes. "This science you so confidently believe in seems equally abstract to me. They're both just ideas that we use to interpret our experience. It seems real to us, simply because we believe it is."

"And?"

"And so the angels are real to me."

"Um."

"Um what?"

"Do you have any chocolate?" We both laugh.

This conversation left me having to interpret everything she said from her religious language to my own under-standing of the world. This language barrier was crossed effectively and I loved our way of talking.

Something in particular happened once which made me realise the significance of our communication. Loz had been involved for sometime with a French church just off Leicester Square and had become friends with a nun there named Jane-Thérèse, after Saint Thérèse of Lisieux. I had been introduced to her and whenever I would see her round the West End I would stop and speak to her. I did not hide anything from her, so talked freely about what I got up to. I wasn't crude but I was honest. It turned out that weeks later, after one of our encounters, that Loz had received a letter from Sister Jane-Thérèse saying. 'Paul makes me sad. Paul makes God sad.' To which Loz had replied by writing, 'Jane-Thérèse, you make God sad.' I had been stood up for, justified in a way that only Loz could. Using her language, both this nun and I were able to understand what was being said. Who were we accountable to, if not ourselves and each other? 'You make God sad.' This made me sad, but only because I thought this a rare understanding.

Loz had promised that she'd do something very special for me. I had asked her to write a letter to my mother if I died. I wanted her to explain in the language my mum understood, what I was all about and even why, if necessary. I felt comfortable that Loz be the voice that I never had with my mother like a link. My mother was very religious. We had begun having communication problems in my teens and although we loved each other, had never been able to get around this. It was more complicated. We had had a break up about five years ago. I had gone to visit her and had felt comfortable telling her about my life. Thinking I had reached a stage where we could just talk as adults. There was too much she didn't want to hear. I was told that I was blaming her for what I had become.

"You're blaming me aren't you? I won't accept that."

"Blaming you for what. You don't understand. I am happy about who I am." I thought I was happy then but this event was to have a lasting affect on me. It was one of the topics I thought had no impact but would cry whenever Gaia asked me about it.

"Why now, after all this time, do you come to tell me all this? You have Aids don't you." At this time I didn't. It was about three years later that I finally contracted HIV.

"No, not that I know of."

Looking back I think this conversation was a lot for my mother to deal with. I had no idea what impact I was having on her. I just wanted to be truthful. I wanted to build some kind of intimacy between us. The situation ended by her striking me and telling me to leave. I thought at the time that I didn't care. She was not a part of my life and now she never would be. I said good-bye to her deep inside. How could I know what it feels like for a mother to hear her son say that he is a prostitute, that he takes drugs and takes risks. How careless could I have been.

I wanted Loz to explain all the sadness I felt, all the love I had. I knew she could do it in a way that would reach my mother, make her proud of me and even feel stronger for what she had learnt. Loz was good at strengthening, more than this I think she was simply good.

I thought a lot about the letter I had received that week and wanted to talk to Gaia about it. I decided to stay in and go to bed early on the Thursday so that I would be able to get to Ladbroke Grove the next day. I even decided not to drink. I knew it would just snowball from there on if I did. I felt terrified whilst trying to sleep that evening. I would start to fall into a nightmare then wake up and be too scared to allow myself to drift off again. I even had to get up and close the bedroom door because I felt so vulnerable. After a couple of hours of torment I took a sleeping tablet, then half an hour later another. Finally it was Friday.

I woke up at eight o'clock that morning and felt unusually excited. It was a similar feeling to staying up late when I was boy. I couldn't remember the last time I had been up that early without it being from the night before and me being at least a little high. It was the heart of spring and such an incredible day. I opened my kitchen window and breathed in. I was suddenly full of confused emotions. I recognised that sense of loss which had so often tried to creep up from within me. It had always been suppressed like the rest of my feelings, except that was when Gaia allowed them free rein. I decided to walk to Ladbroke Grove that morning. It was a long walk but I felt up to it and had plenty of time. I walked through Holland Park, in between the aisle of huge chestnuts that line the main pathway. The feelings I had felt in the kitchen returned but stronger and even more mixed-up. There was one feeling which seemed to love everything in an over excited way. This was uncomfortable, making me nervous and wary. Then there was the feeling that I was missing out on something very special in life. The last thing I recognised from within this whirl, was hate. I was going to die of Aids, that's if the drugs didn't get me first.

"Is this all I'll ever have?" I said to myself in a whisper. To which I replied. "It's all you're worth." My eyes started to water. A bird's song burst into this misery which brought on intense love again and around my mind span with my feelings in tow. By the time I reached Gaia I felt drained and numb. I told her about all the confusion.

She sat with the tips of her fingers covering her mouth. Then slowly she began to speak. "It's as though you are waking to see all these beautiful things and you're stopping yourself because you're scared of what you might feel, perhaps even scared that you'll feel too much."

I wanted to talk about the letter. I didn't want to hear what she had to say about that morning. I had only wanted to get it out.

She continued ". . .and I can't help being reminded of how you stopped yourself feeling when you last spoke to Kevin." I knew what she was saying was making sense but I hardly registered it. Maybe I wasn't ready to hear it yet.

I don't remember what else, if anything, was covered that day. Sometimes I was so tightly shut even Gaia couldn't get in. At least that's what appeared was happening. I still had the letter from Loz in my mind. Where was this place that was not with her? Did I really care? Did I choose to be where I was? If I did why? Although Gaia didn't deal directly with any of these thoughts she did respond to my feelings. Indirectly she helped me by being with me, by sometimes being parts of me, sometimes being my mum, but that day by being a Loz with whom I hadn't lost my link. As she talked about feeling too much and Kevin and whatever

35

else, I felt good in her room, having the company of her. I decided that I wanted to see Loz, to talk properly, so I planned to call her.

I later learnt that there was a name for what happened that day. It was referred to as transference, the process of projecting people in ones life onto the therapist. This interested me less than the fact that I felt an inkling of harmony, at least in one area of my life. Even when I understood what was happening I still used it because I liked it, or needed it. As time went by, the whole therapy process quickened. I felt I began to understand how Gaia processed what I told her. So I began to link ideas by myself. She would sometimes smile in agreement or look confused as she pondered what I suggested. I also began to relate to her way of looking at things, but I was determined to remember that it was only 'one' way of looking at things. I didn't want to be consumed by her.

CHAPTER SEVEN

Another month passed and with it several Friday mornings. 'I didn't drink again last night,' was becoming my regular opening line.

I still got drunk often, but not on a Thursday night. If I didn't drink then I managed not to take drugs and so got a good night's sleep. This was useful for me, not just in relation to being able to get to therapy, but also because regular sleep made me feel so much more sane. I felt a lot healthier. I was eating more and put on weight. As healthy as I became, a day didn't pass without me thinking about the virus inside me. I did feel better about it, but it still meant so much. My drug taking was down to about once a week. Sometimes I even went without for a couple of weeks at a time.

My mother was the topic of the hour this particular morning. I tried to change the direction of the conversation but was brought directly back to it. Outwardly I switched off and stared at my feet, but this tactic didn't work either.

"You seem to feel uncomfortable talking about your mother." That's right, I thought, let it drop. "Could you tell me about this?" My reply was to continue staring at my feet, but now it was because I was confused. I had felt uncomfortable, she was right, although I hadn't realised this until she pointed it out.

"She's not a big part of my life, there's not much to say." I forced myself to confront what I might be harbouring.

"Why do you think she's not a big part of your life?"

I was reluctant to even think about this subject but I decided to try and answer her. "I told you about our argument, before."

"Yes and how do you feel about it?"

"I don't really care."

"Are you saying you don't care about your mother or the argument or you don't care what happens now?"

"I still can't forgive her for doing what she did."

"Tell me again how you felt when she told you to leave."

37

"I felt that she didn't want me there anymore." I said this as though what I was saying was so obvious.

"Are you saying that you felt rejected?"

"I guess so." It was only now that I heard what I had said. I had known the answer but I hadn't realised the significance of it. I had actually felt something and it was likely that I still did.

The conversation only led this far at that time, but it was picked up on again at a later date. In between I got a phone call from my sister Helen, asking if she could visit. She was on her way to the wedding anniversary of an old friend. It seemed soon, considering my brother had visited a year earlier. After he left I thought it was clear that he had been sent down to see if I was well. I'm sure if I had looked sick I would have had the whole family on my case in seconds. I had actually just got over amoebic dysentery but because of this I had been resting up for a week. The doctor had prescribed an anti-amoebic medicine, on which if you drink, you are violently sick. I had lost weight but at least I was coherent.

Helen arrived with her husband to whom I was polite but not particularly friendly. After making coffee and settling, my sister asked if I would go with her to the shop to get some cigarettes. I guessed what she was up to, so went along with it. As soon as we got out of the door she looked at me very bravely and said. "Why don't you ever visit?"

"You know why. I just don't feel like seeing mum." I had thought about this enough to feel confident of what I said.

"If it's because of the fight, don't you think it's about time..?"

"What? About time she said sorry? That's not even what I want. I just can't believe she did that to me. How can I forgive her?"

"Because she's a different generation, because she loves you and was upset. How many reasons do you want?"

Feeling confused I moaned, "I don't care." As I said this it didn't ring true, even to me. I began to think of what Gaia had said about pretending. We walked in silence for a while, then, as though timed to perfection, Helen stepped

38

in front of me just before entering my flat. As though this were the last second outside reality, away from the man inside who represented a different kind of family life that I couldn't possibly relate to. She looked me straight in the eye again which she knew was her vantage point.

"Do you really not care?" She knew that the slightest twitch of my eye would give everything away. She got what she wanted. I turned away. Helen got hold of my face with her hand and kissed me on my cheek.

"I love you, you silly thing and so does mum."

I told her that I'd follow her in. I had to get my head together before her husband saw me.

That night, after Helen left, I got very drunk and ended up in a dark corner of Queer getting sick on ecstasy. It seemed as though even drugs wouldn't help me lie any longer. Lola was under the stairs. It all seemed too hideously predictable. I left. I called Josie and went round in a cab. For some reason I started to talk about Kevin again. Everything upsetting from my recent past and some way before seemed to come pouring out that day. I went to the toilet and realised that I had shat in my underpants. I couldn't help laughing at myself for doing this. Josie found it funny too. Eventually I fell asleep on the sofa with my head on her lap. When I woke up Josie told me that I had fallen asleep crying and that she had put my underpants and jeans in the washing machine. All I remember is that I was warm and Josie was kind. One minute it was Sunday morning, the next it was evening. I had taken four temazepam and fallen asleep soon after swallowing them. So often I wondered what I would do without sleeping tablets. Sometimes the need to be asleep was so necessary, I think I would have done whatever it took to stop myself being conscious. Their effect could be so instant, especially if I took enough. I was once walking on my knees to turn off the television set and never made it. I woke up literally with my arm still reaching for the on-off button. The kind of sleep I got when so drugged never felt real, it seemed more like a switching off. I guess this is why sometimes I woke-up in the same position as I had fallen asleep in. Once this happened while

I was fucking someone, whilst actually inside them. In the morning he had gone. I can't help wondering what he must have felt, realising that I was slowing down, then stopping but not starting again. He must have had to push me off. It must have been a difficult task, lying on his front under someone a lot bigger than himself. Then how must he have felt getting dressed and leaving. I do remember that we had used a condom and that it was gone in the morning so he must have taken it off me and got rid of it. I thought this very polite. He's never spoken to me since.

It seemed as though I spent a lot of time crying in those days, but these tears weren't all the same. From my conversations with Gaia I endeavoured to categorised them into three types: There was, life's a mess, nothing goes right for me. These can be seen as self indulgent. Then, oh how beautiful I can hardly believe such things exist. These happen at movies when two lovers are finally together again or good conquers evil. Finally there are uncontrollable child-like tears of pure emotion. These come gushing out when Gaia manages to make me really feel something. This last kind are refreshing and feel very healthy.

After drugs especially between Monday and Wednesday I would cry at literally anything. I didn't know why it happened but I knew it happened to other people too. Josie had coined these as 'chemical tears'. They included all types but were exaggerated because of a hypersensitivity due to drug withdrawal.

"Why do we cry?" I said to Gaia one day. "Does it do any good?"

"We have tear-ducts for a reason," she replied, smiling, presumably at the simplicity of it. I laughed. It did seem that simple. Of course there was a purpose to it. Of course it did some good. Gaia then explained that you can cry from in the valley as you see what's all around you. Or you can cry from the hilltop as you see what's below, aware that you're free of it all, yet it was a part of your life. Now I felt I understood my tears, and this made me cry again.

During our sessions we decided that some subjects were more pressing and that others had to wait. The drugs were quite an immediate issue and were being dealt with slowly. I had always taken drugs. Whilst at school I smoked cannabis which my friend had grown in his bedroom. We would sniff poppers, drink cider and get stoned. When I left home at about eighteen I started taking speed, which became a weekly thing, along with lots of alcohol. There was a gap of a few years as I went through college. I always drank a lot but the drugs didn't start again until I returned to London and was introduced to ecstasy, acid and cocaine. I started jacking up in the last couple of years.

Gaia never actually said much about the drugs directly. She did suggest that I might be trying to numb myself and that more recently it may be specifically related to my HIV status. Gaia suggested that I might also have a lot of guilt. As always I tried to leave myself open to all of the links that she made. I was taking less drugs. I don't understand why the process she used worked, but it did seem to, at least as regards to this. I was constantly questioning the whole notion of therapy. I justified it by telling myself that there was probably no harm in it. Although I wasn't even sure about this. I remember thinking that I should be cautious. I'm not sure if I thought I could be locked away as insane, or just scared that my mind could actually be tampered with by someone else.

Along with the drugs came an abuse tendency which expressed itself through violent or aggressive sex, generally where I was restrained, degraded or physically violated. This was also expressed within my friendships, playing out roles, hurting and being hurt, controlling and being controlled. It was much more noticeable within my sex life and exaggerated greatly when on drugs. This is where we began looking at this. For now it was being linked with drugs because taking them facilitated a definite outlet. Gaia suggested that the taking of the drugs to begin with was yet another way of abusing myself.

I had met a man in New York four years earlier at the end of December who introduced me to sado-masochistic sex. I was visiting a sugar-daddy punter at the time called Gregory. I had never really liked the idea of sugar-daddies

41

because I didn't like lying and as a rule wouldn't be false. If I liked someone I certainly wouldn't ask them to pay me for my time and if I didn't why would they possibly want to spend time with someone who didn't want to be with them. Gregory was special though, he was extremely bright and seemed to have a good grasp of what was between us. We talked and he seemed genuinely interested, thinking I had gone astray and that he could help me. We never had sex, which I felt meant he respected the fact that I didn't find him attractive. I did really like him. Gregory avoided leading a gay lifestyle.

"When I see them marching every year, I don't feel proud. Why do they behave like that?"

"It's only a bit of fun."

"I don't see why they have to behave any different from everyone else."

"I guess it's because that's how we've always been treated."

"All that screaming and shouting." Gregory had entered his own world by now and was neither listening or caring what I thought of what he was saying. This world must have been safer for him, more sympathetic.

"I think there's good reason to shout."

"How will gays ever be accepted if they don't integrate?"

"*They*," I thought, but felt there was something too fragile about his irritation to confront him.

He wanted children and I think he would have made a thoughtful father. He would happily get married to do this. I don't think this would have been fair to any woman or to himself. As controlled as he could be, I thought if he attempted this, someday something would have to give. To me, Gregory was only sweet and kind. With me, I guess he got as near as he ever had to being honest about his true feelings. I could tell that he enjoyed giving me things and I generally enjoyed receiving them. Our weekends were spent shopping or sight-seeing and in the evenings we'd eat in smart Manhattan restaurants or go to the theatre. Christmas made it magical. Americans seemed to put so much more energy into Christmas, giving gifts to each other to show they care. This seemed particularly important to Gregory. I don't think this generosity was a substitute for kindness. We flew over the city in a helicopter, together enjoying the wintry view. The millions of tiny lights made me feel as though I was special. I felt he cared about me to do all this for me.

During the weekdays Gregory went out early to work leaving me to spend the days how ever I wanted. I worked out at the YMCA, walked in Central Park, went to the little zoo there and discovered the cruising area. I was casually followed and finally spoken to by a man who took me back to his apartment on the West Side, only one block up from where I was staying. He gave me acid and some Quaaludes. He ended up tying me up, pissing on me, slapping me and trying to stick his fist up my arse. Thinking about it the following week I decided that I had enjoyed it or rather I got something from it, although I didn't know exactly what. We kept in contact as he often visited London. Our relationship developed and became what he wanted, he had a clearer vision than I. He enjoyed dominating me. He made me drink his piss. He spat on me. He made me sit on his big dick which hurt a lot. He would position us in front of a mirror so that I would have to watch myself be humiliated. This was the most difficult thing to do. He would put his dirty underwear in my mouth and call me his little whore. I couldn't believe at the time how little physical pleasure I got out of this. There was always a feeling that maybe any minute it might happen. On one level I would literally beg him for more, on another I wanted a different kind of love and affection. Well aware of what I wanted he would slap me hard around the face. If I moved away or even winced he'd start to walk away saying, "You shit, why do I bother with you?"

I would grab hold of him.

"Ah, you want me to stay. You like what I do to you don't you?"

Then he would hit me again and again until I answered.

"Yes." Now that I was broken and soft, instantly he changed.

43

"My baby's hurt. I love you but you've got to behave."

This must have been what I waited for because it was tender and real and so close to love.

I went home to London and carried on my life. Then several months later Gregory came to town and arranged to meet me in the restaurant at the Savoy. Everything had changed. He had so much contempt for me, verging on hatred. He said that I hadn't taken responsibility for my actions and that he had fallen in love with me. As far as he was concerned prostitution was bad, because it hurt him and had made me too callous to notice. What he didn't realise is that I could clearly see his pain, although I didn't feel I was to blame. He was looking for love in a strange place. We had already set up an imbalance of power in both directions. Can love grow within this? Gregory wanted a wife and a family. He looked for it in a whore, who was a boy, who wanted so many things but not the rules that he had run away from all his life. Discovering he wasn't getting what he wanted, Gregory didn't realise why? He must have thought that, in time, if he was nice to me, I would have fallen in love with him. Even I knew that it just doesn't happen like that. It's a shame because I could have and probably would have grown to love him. Maybe this wouldn't have been enough. So the finger was pointed at me and I was all evil. A prostitute is such an easy target. He fell for this idea and focused his attack on it. He eloquently and single-mindedly crushed me into silence. We were served scones and tea. Gregory loved clotted cream. The whole event took about an hour and a half. Finally I left feeling confused and very cruel.

During my sessions with Gaia, prostitution featured highly. It was a complicated, possibly deeper part of my life, which seemed to be linked to everything I did. A lot of Gaia's work was about helping me to link things. I had a tendency to separate everything in life. Like sex and emotion, cause and expression of anger, even reality and fantasy.

I always liked to use the word 'prostitution' for the job I did, although lots of other words were used. 'Rent-boy' seems to me to conjure up images of teenagers on the street who had run away from home. I had worked on the street but anyone who had any sense could get it together to put an ad in a gay paper so as not have to stand around in the cold. The word 'hooker' reminded me of leggy, skimpily dressed American women from early evening, t.v. detective shows. Hustler was the one I really disliked. It seemed so moralistic as though anyone who did the job would steal from you, mug you, or generally rip you off. This seemed so far from the truth as I can't remember how many times punters have tried to mistreat me or get away without paying. I've even had them say 'I'll give you more if we can have unsafe sex'. Elsewhere in life I don't often encounter such evil at first hand. The terms 'escort' and 'masseur' I find a joke, that people need use such euphemisms to help themselves deal with the work they do. 'Prostitute' is the word I like, I feel like it says: 'Do you have a problem with that?' Which is how I like to approach it. Although not always, mothers don't seem to take to it.

Prostitution has affected me, everything does on some level. People generally assume that it makes one disconnect emotion and sex. If this is true, I have to ask myself: Did prostitution create the disconnecting or did notions that I already had make prostitution suitable for me? Gaia suggests that it was probably a bit of both and whichever it was, the disconnection is likely to have been compounded. I think it probably has different effects on each individual. I'm still working on it. People have often asked me does it get confusing? How can I tell the difference between sex with punters and sex for fun? I usually ask them to imagine what it would feel like to have thousands of men mauling them whom they found repulsive, then to imagine how different it would feel to have someone touch them who they liked. If anything I found it made it more clear. I can't help joking that it would be handy not to be able to tell them apart and then get paid for having fun. I'm finding as I get older that I have to be turned on to someone mentally. I can swoon if a man says the right thing to me. This can range from . . . 'I can't wait to see you, kiss you and hold you,' through to . . . 'Lick my boots and shut the fuck up.' It's about showing an understanding of intensity. I get off on the fact that my partner might be bright enough to pick-up on and then be bothered enough to give me what I want. In an odd kind of way it appears to show that they care. Good looks alone don't necessarily turn me on, in fact I have found having sex with repulsive men very exciting. This is because it feels so self-abasing. As a prostitute I have been continually worshipped physically, so on one level I think I like degradation just because it's a change. I have found it difficult getting people to do this to me.

I met an alcoholic once who suggested that prostitution had made me loose my self-respect. He had come across this idea as part of his twelve step program offered at AA. I slowly began to relate to this, not realising that it might not be relevant. Eventually I interpreted a great deal of my thoughts and feelings to fit in with what he had said. It was only as my drug and alcohol habits eased, that I realised that my insecurities may be related to chemical addiction and not prostitution at all. I'd hate to think that I had made a mistake all these years and prostitution had really fucked me up. I knew that it had brought about changes in my life but I found the changes interesting. I would like to believe prostitution a valid occupation whatever the general morality on the subject is. As far as what the law says, it proves itself to be insensitive about too many things, if not completely unjust and bad.

CHAPTER EIGHT

Sometimes things happened which made me notice that there had been changes in my life. It was getting on to autumn and like many gay men I had pictures of cuddling up in bed with some lovely boy not wanting to get up to coldness. In dreams, I spent the whole day in bed, rubbing my cold nose against his warm lips, snug from the heat of him. It was in this frame of mind that I noticed a somebody in a bar one night. I watched him for some time and was impressed by how he moved, spoke to his friends, smiled and more than occasionally looked over at me. I saw him head towards the toilet and was wondering how I could cut him off on the way back. A crowd of my friends came in and I was distracted enough not to see where he had gone. I thought he might have gone to the toilet so decided to follow and possibly talk to him. As I turned round I was face to face with a beautiful sight. He was there, right behind me. He had come over to talk to me.

"Oh, sorry, I didn't realise you were with friends."

"I'm not . . . I mean they're not my friends. What I mean is . . . I hadn't planned to meet them." We both laughed at my clumsy explanation. "I'd rather talk to you is what I mean. They'll understand if they're any friends at all."

At this point I was handed a drink and sure enough was left alone.

"Considerate friends," he said.

"Yeah. What's your name?"

"Daniel."

This is how the conversation went, nothing special, but nice all the same. We arranged a date at the weekend and went to see a film. I felt as though he liked me, but sure enough, later on in the evening he told me that he had a boyfriend. He asked if we could still get together so I told him to phone me. I wanted time to think about it. Just as I began persuading myself that, maybe he wasn't close to his boyfriend, or maybe they were breaking up, Daniel called me.

47

"I mentioned your name to Jason, my partner and he knows you. He said you spoke to him at ff a few weeks ago and you planned to go home with him." Unusual as it was, I could remember who he was talking about and I did want to sleep with him.

"Oh he's your boyfriend, that's a coincidence."

"Well we've been talking and we wondered if you would like to come round for dinner some night." I interpreted this as we'd like to sandwich you. I had known from experience that with boyfriends one was generally more active and one more passive, so in a three way situation the newcomer was often in the middle. I happened to love this, so felt quite excited at the prospect of going round for dinner with them.

"I'm not quite sure, um. Are you sure you're both cool about it?" What I meant by this was, had they done it before and did it work out okay. There had been occasions in the past where one would get jealous if I spent too much time with the other. Then I would have to concentrate more on the one feeling left out. On drugs this could get really confusing and twisted. I also might start feeling neglected. On the other hand, it if it went well it could be great fun.

"Yeah, we both think you're really cute. It'll be hot."

"Okay. When?"

So we arranged the date, although I still felt unsure. Maybe them not being able to handle it wasn't the only problem.

It went like clockwork, the foreplay, the sandwich, even the dinner yet I came away feeling that something was wrong. A week later Daniel telephoned wanting to do it all over again. I told him that I would rather do it just with him and that I didn't really fancy his boyfriend. Of course, like most boyfriends, he agreed, and arranged it for the next time Jason was out of town. I suspected not fancying Jason wasn't really the problem. Daniel picked me up and took me to his house. As we went through his front door I was pushed against the wall and kissed violently. Ideas flashed into my mind. Is this what I'm giving off? Am I constantly inviting harsh treatment? We seemed to move in one fluid motion from the hall to the bed, squashing me underneath him. He held my arms above my head, firmly staked by his huge hands and stuck his tongue deep inside my mouth. As he pulled out, he lifted his torso up over me, hovered, then lowered himself down and pressed his crotch into my face. This felt predictable but at the same time sent a spark deep into my stomach and seemed to prickle something in my balls. Holding my wrists with just one hand and the heavy weight of his body, he opened his fly and groped for his dick. Taking it in his hand he pulled it out. It was warm and smooth and smelt incredible. He pushed it up against my nose and in the sockets of my eyes. This felt reassuring. I understood his teasing so kept my mouth closed but I couldn't help but nuzzle round his shaft, his hair and balls. Again the smell reached far inside me, overriding consciousness and thoughts. His softness and hardness turned me inside out. I became consumed, physical and responsive, sensitive and lost. Now his dick prodded my mouth, lifting and teasing, pre-cum sticking and wetting. I wanted so bad to lick my lips, to open and swallow the whole of him. The grinding action of his hips pushed his dick slowly inside my mouth, not stopping to rest, but straight on down to the back of my throat. Daniel groaned, 'Jesus Christ.' I wasn't going to stop him and I loved his response, him loving the feeling I gave him. All I wanted was him to carry on, to keep giving me the ability to give. Fucking and fucking he attacked my throat, so much pain and all I wanted was him to carry on. I freed one hand and tried to control his hammering, but he seemed to only go faster with more aggression. I reached for my own dick and pulled it free from being wrapped, so hard, in cotton and pre-cum, so swollen and desperate and aching. I jerked and was taken further into the scene, now right with him, as far gone and mean. My own excitement allowed me more, to except more of what he was giving. Now so close myself, I let go of my dick and got my hand around his arse and it was perfect and pumping and loving me, so smooth and solid and mine. I forced him against me harder and harder. He loved this and so did I. "Fucking yeah, baby." He laughed and moaned, getting faster and

49

wilder and ramming and ramming so far in, then crying, 'fucking hell.' He spasmed and jolted and froze where he was, as he burst in my mouth and came and came. I shook and trembled, swallowed and choked, my dick squirting as I gasped for air. I could smell his cum. I could taste his cum as I fell back into my life. Daniel stayed just where he was for several perfect minutes, his sweaty crotch spreading his cum over my now slimy face. I was happy. Pulling out of my mouth he rolled over, then jumped up with a smile and a wink, then gestured some kind of washing action and headed towards the bathroom. A soon as we were showered he said, "Do you mind if I take you home now." I didn't turn around or respond. "It's just that I've got a meeting first thing tomorrow. I've got to get an early start." I thought this so clichéd. I suddenly felt uncomfortable. There had been something weird from the beginning for me. Firstly because I liked him. This may have only been because I felt degraded. Secondly because I wanted him to respect me and cared that he didn't. Lastly because I became aware that I wanted something else, something a little more connected. This was one of those changes. I was beginning to want respect. It crept up on me, and there it was demanding a voice, and all it took was a certain situation at the right time to make me see it clearly. So maybe I did want to feel liked by those I had sex with. Possibly I wanted to like them too. I could see from this that if I wasn't careful I might become vulnerable, opening myself up to all kinds of nonsense.

CHAPTER NINE

I was still meeting Josie every Friday and sometimes on Tuesdays. I had begun the twice weekly therapy sessions in August. Gaia had wanted this from the beginning but I hadn't liked the idea of spending that much time with her. She suggested that the sessions would link more easily and that there would be less pressure on the Friday session. The first time I went on the Tuesday I felt uncomfortable, so presumed that it was probably the right decision.

I saw my male friends more than I saw Josie. Like many gay men I spent a lot of my time doing things that involved looking for or having sex. When it came to this and also making money, Josie's and my live's became very separate. In her case that was her love life and her career. Josie had been seeing a woman for the last year called Maire. This was new for her, before this she had only dated men. Josie put time and energy into this relationship. Maire had a daughter which tended to ground them both to a certain extent.

Josie always seemed to be doing something interesting. Sometimes organising exhibitions, styling fashion shows, writing songs or film scripts, all sorts of things. The link was that whatever she did it was generally creative. She was well known and popular, so I felt as though I had to earn the time I spent with her.

There were few women in my life but the ones that were seem to affect me so much. Loz had a way of touching my soul before I even knew I had one. My mother hurt me as only she could. Gaia made me cry from sadness and joy. Josie simply offered me solace.

I found my therapist through a woman doctor. When she first asked did it matter what sex my therapist was, I said yes. I wanted a gay man, preferably one who was HIV positive. My temporary counsellor was, as requested, a man, but also a goblin type figure who suggested that my frequent nose blowing was a way of trying to purge myself. I explained that I had a cold and that my sinuses were probably damaged from constantly snorted drugs.

One day he used the word 'shit' which seemed very self-conscious and contrived. I couldn't take him seriously after that. I changed my mind about wanting a male therapist. I lucked out and got Gaia who says that it might have been what I was looking for all along, a safe and positive relationship with a women.

My man I met in Central Park came into town in November. Since I had met him I had only seen him six times. He was staying at a hotel but spent a lot of time round at my flat. I had been avoiding having sex with him all week, with the excuse that I didn't want to take drugs. I put it off until the weekend. I knew he had to leave on the Monday. A part of me did want to get close to him and please him, but I knew what I would have to put up with to get there. We decided to meet in a leather bar that I sometimes went to. It was easier to go there and not get too wasted but still pick up. I went with Marcus who wore chaps, a harness, a dog collar and lead. He looked so sweet. No girls were allowed and there was a strict dress code: leather, uniform and no strong smelling after-shave. They allowed a leather jacket and jeans as long as it was masculine looking, nothing fashiony or camp. I got very drunk and then was easily persuaded to take some speed, acid and ecstasy. A perfect combination for long, nasty sado-masochistic sex. I began to feel a bit wasted so went upstairs to a dark, quiet corner. I sat on a table with my hands on my knees. I was looking at the ground trying to concentrate on where I was and what I was doing. This focusing was a way of getting my head together. I thought, okay, you're out of it, what are you going to do? I decided that I needed some more speed. I couldn't help noticing a dust ball about a foot long on the floor rolling in front of me. I was surprised that there was a draft, but not that there was a dust ball on a beer sodden busy walkway. As I watched it rose up and started to weave in and out of itself, bands of rainbow rays folded and unfolded. The ribbons of dust sat in the air pulsating. I half understood what was happening and realised it wasn't a dust ball after all. It must just be the way the dim coloured lights are catching the air. This made complete sense at the time, until I told Marcus who burst out laughing. I found him on his knees in the middle of the dance floor. Yes and I ended up back with the American before I knew it. He went further than he ever had before. When he had finished, which was when he was exhausted, I couldn't sleep. I asked if I could call a friend. He told me to shut up and lie still. The next day, in the evening, we began play fighting and somehow it escalated to a wavering border between fun and violence. I was used to fighting, it had always played a part in my life. It seemed to me that to be good at it, to win that was, it took three things. One was, to think quickly, even when frightened. The other to remember moves, what worked and what didn't. Finally and probably the most important was to be determined. This last device was what I used in this instance. With all my strength I managed to pin him down. I remember staring down at his face, looking so pathetic and defeated and weak. With every attempt he made to buck me off I became more angry and more determined. There was a moment where I think I scared him and if I didn't then he was a fool.

"What am I becoming? This isn't how I want to behave. It's not what I want to be. Someone who fights because they can't say what they mean."

"But you were saying something, weren't you?"

"The worst thing is I don't feel bad about it. I feel justified somehow." I was confused as always but I didn't feel wrong.

"I think maybe you had had enough. I think that maybe you wanted to stop the abuse and you spoke with violence."

I began to cry and it was from the hillside as I saw what I had been a part of. I had done something about it, all by myself, without completely understanding. Gaia was there as always to hand me the piece of the puzzle that I had missed. As I left that day I said thank-you. I think she knew what I meant.

That night I had a wet dream. I woke up with a hard on. The whole series of events was clear in my head. I had been fantasising about a man I had never met. It was the boyfriend of this same man I had fought. I had been told that his boyfriend liked to be tied up and abused but that my guy couldn't do it to him for some reason. I think it might have been because he cared about him. I had this boyfriend tied face down on a bed, his arms and legs stretched apart. It was in their home, I recognised some of his things. I was kneeling in between his legs looking at the crack of his arse. I fucked him against his will as he pleaded with me to stop. I lay onto his back and whispered in his ear that I wasn't wearing a condom and that I was going to cum up his arse. He was crying but I kept fucking. When I came I kissed him and comforted him and told him that I had been safe. He continued to cry but he was happy and wanted my comforting. I untied him and held him. He was beautifully soft and hurt. I wrapped myself around him to keep him warm and kissed him until he fell asleep.

It seemed clear from this that Gaia had been right. I did know both, sadistic and masochistic roles. I thought my dream was a retaliation, doing to him, or what he loved most, what he did to me. I may have been reading the dream in this way because Gaia suggested this was what was happening. More subtly, I may have only remembered what I wanted to remember. The thing that was clear is that there had been a change. I was getting in touch with different aspects of myself. This I think was a good thing, although it certainly didn't seem like it at times.

CHAPTER TEN

I spent the following week by myself, so had lots of time to think. It was clear to me that something was happening. I understood some areas of my life more and more, at least from the perspective of psychotherapy. I wrote a letter to Loz.

Dear Loz,

There are times, like now, when I feel so much. It seems more complex than simply happy and sad. This is probably because I'm too involved in it to understand. I hate something. I miss something, so I pine for something. I respect myself enough to be angry but my direction is so unclear.

I calm myself and try to focus, but this is only a construction, something put on top, at best a stepping stone, under which lies crackling legs and impenetrable boned casing, using me to breed beneath.

I'm not going to fake anything. I am already too disappointed to do this to myself. It's just so hard to know what is true. There is so much turmoil that I've become resigned to it. I now have a deformed understanding through which I see, hear and remember my life.

I can screen my real self, but I can't replace it.

Paul.

I felt a mild depression, which wasn't something I was particularly prone to. After trying to decide who or what was the cause, I asked vaguely, "What is depression?"

Gaia pursed her lips ever so slightly. "I see it as a holding down of something. I think maybe its a holding down of

55

emotions and thoughts." With this she made the action with her hands as though she were pushing something from her chest to the level of her abdomen. "As in depress. You could look at it as a device for keeping things in a place where they don't have to be dealt with."

I listened and watched with fascination, and I think because of this she smiled her smile. For me Gaia had just turned it all on it's head. I thought depression was a cause rather than a reaction. She was suggesting that it was an indication. It seemed ironic but I guessed it was therapy that was causing my depression. I was being made aware of aspects of myself, but that didn't necessarily mean I was able to confront them. I knew that even if I did, healing wasn't instant, but more a merging of ideas and possibly some eventual change.

My letter to Loz acted for me as a discharge. It also let her know that I was thinking, and by this, that I was trying to get to a place that she knew. A letter from her arrived within days. I fancied she had sat down and replied with my letter still held in one of her hands.

Dearest Paul,

Give yourself a rest, you are fighting with the depths.

Love
Loz.

I think I knew what she meant. I had a familiar 'I don't want to deal with it' feeling. It was uncomfortable because it was a reminder.

It was the Friday of this week that I told Josie about the chaotic state of my mind.

Pulling out a spoon from her mouth, on it the remains of chocolate mousse, she held up her finger and nodded, to get my attention. Then waiting for barely a minute for her mouthful to dissolve she asked in a casual but equally definite way, "Have you ever thought about meditation?"

"What?" This was very new to me, so much so, that I

wasn't quite sure she had said what she had.

"Transcendental meditation." Then not getting a reply, she asked again. "Have you ever thought about it?" My answer was a jumbled mutter. "Do you know what it is?"

"No, I don't think I do."

Josie began to elaborate, telling me how she had first come across it, how she had practised it and even what use she thought it had been. I was surprised that she hadn't told me about it before, but as she pointed out, we hadn't really known each other very long. This thoughtful person was giving me a gift. In an understated manner she was giving me something she thought very important. We had had to get this far in our relationship before she felt it the right thing to do. Looking back I think it was much more timely than either of us could have known.

A week later Josie phoned. I would have happily forgotten about our conversation. She gave me the telephone number of the man who had taught her TM. He was expecting me to call, and all I had to do was introduce myself. I phoned and arranged to visit him. I was told to bring along five white flowers, three pieces of fruit, but not grapefruit, and a white handkerchief. I turned up without these things explaining that I didn't see why the ceremony was necessary. From what I understood, meditation was a state of mind and body. Why the mysticism? My teacher, a middle aged man with long permed silver hair, looked as guru-like as he possibly could. I was left alone to watch a video while he went about running his business. The video was one man's explanation of TM metaphysics and how everything was intrinsically linked. The camera kept zooming in and out. I guessed for dramatic effect. The man was sweating and for some reason he appeared to want to give his speech all in one go. This entailed constant stopping to look at notes, repetition and lots of fidgeting. These distractions only served to fill in the time during his long winded explanation. His point made, my TM teacher came back into the room and asked me what I thought. After I told him he said, "You're not interested are you? Why did you come? Did Josie drag you here?"

"No she didn't. She suggested it. I am interested but it just seems like there's so much surrounding this that I can't deal with." I knew by this stage to blame it on myself before he got too upset. I didn't want to get Josie into trouble.

"Maybe you're just not ready for it yet."

I sat silently for I was disappointed that I hadn't got more out of it. "Yeah, maybe I could call you another time when I think I'm more ready." I didn't want to give up so easily, but I couldn't bear all this man stood for.

"Some people don't seem to appreciate what I'm offering them. He obviously found me easy prey. He vented his anger by giving me other examples of similar situations. I was screaming inside to get away from him. I thought the hallway would be my salvation. I had my hand on the front door ready to escape when he asked could he have a lift up the street. He had a captive audience for the next five minutes. As he talked I could see his long filed nails waving around beside me followed by flashes of white embroidered muslin. I felt wound up and twisted out of myself by the time I got home. This was my introduction to TM.

Josie was very good about it all, laughing as I relayed the story. This man had been right for her, so I tried to respect this, again putting more emphasis on my failings. It was only a few days later that I received another call from Josie who had already tracked down another teacher. Even though they had not met, Josie was excited because she had read a book of hers. It would cost one hundred pounds to be taught by her. Her name was Nancy. I loved this name. I had a beautiful aunt called Nancy. Also I had once met a waitress with this name. My job was washing dishes, one of the only legal jobs I ever had. She told me that I was well adjusted. I was so surprised that someone so bright and gorgeous and so comfortable in her surroundings could think this of me. I got the sack. This happened every time I had a job. It was so humiliating. Nancy helped me see that I was only a little bit of what I could be. I lost contact with her. As soon as I did I started hoping that I'd find her again some day.

I telephoned my new teacher and spoke to her. I was

told I would need the same things as before, the flowers and so on.

"Josie told me about the obstacles encountered last time. Let me start by explaining what these gifts are for. They're to give thanks to all the teachers that have gone before us, including the Maharishi himself." There was a few seconds silence before she said, ". . .yes?"

I pictured her raising her eyebrows and lifting up her chin, as her 'yes' I guessed was a question. I understood this as, "Do you understand?" So I also said yes.

"You don't have to believe in any of this. I'm simply going to teach you a technique you might find useful for the rest of your life."

I couldn't help butting in at this point. "This is what I want." I loved the sound of her voice, she had a strong American accent. I got the address of her home and arranged to see her four days later.

I called a punter who I could rely upon at times like this when I needed extra money. I saved him for special occasions because servicing him got so complicated. I had to use a catheter, but this was only the beginning, he was very particular. Wearing long rubber gloves I would arrange glass bottles, various sizes, for collecting his specimens. I understood his fantasy as somewhere between medical examinations and regular water sports. I really couldn't comprehend the place he went to, so wasn't with him anymore than being a bystander, keeping him company. I was sure there were reasons so I couldn't help guessing. Was I the voyeur in this scene and not just an assistant? Maybe I was several things besides these. Things that I wouldn't feel comfortable with, if I knew. The muscles in his face would get so busy, possibly showing his ideas, constructing, pausing, adding, and then swapping this for that. I really don't know. I wasn't invited inside his head. And yes, I even imagined my exclusion might be part of his fetish.

I decided to buy white roses, red apples and I borrowed a handkerchief from Marcus's collection. Nancy was the picture of an ideal of mine. She reclined on a sofa opposite

59

me. Her blonde hair was pulled into curvy shapes, nestling behind her Versace medallion earrings. Comfort and glamour I think were her goals and she achieved them. Nancy was a widow who appeared to live comfortably, so I guessed teaching gave pin money. I didn't resent her at all. She spoke mainly in anecdotes about herself and her famous friends. It all seemed dull to me but I liked her for liking her life. I'm sure she was able to charm any host and was given things for just being her. Nancy appeared to be successful. What I mean by this is that I felt that she was good at life, good at living.

Nancy took me into a box room. It was simple with a little altar. Nancy performed a ceremony and then gave me my mantra. I was told it should never be spoken aloud once learnt. To meditate I had to repeat this in my head. I did this for twenty minutes and felt as though I really got something out of it. I saw Nancy one more time and found that when I meditated with her it felt good.

What I found strange was I seemed to separate my thoughts into two different kinds. At least this is how I understood it for the purpose of meditation. If I was to say a word, my mantra, inside my head, I found I could also start day-dreaming pictures. I was told that if I found myself thinking of something else I should just remind myself to go back to my mantra. If I pictured the mantra as I imagined it to be spelt, it seemed to leave less room for other images or spoken words to come into my mind. Nancy told me that men have a tendency to be aggressive about keeping to their mantra, but the ideal is to let it be itself, let it become a whisper then a mere thread of a conscious word or thing. The goal was to reach a place where this thread becomes a plateau of the unconscious where neither sound nor images exist any longer.

As time went by in my meditation, I would drift from the conscious, easily and often, to where, I don't know. It were as though I would switch off. This was not sleep, I think, for I would have no recollection of dreams or ideas. Sometimes when I came out from it, I felt as though I had been dead. I don't understand it very well. Gaia listened as

I told her but had nothing to say about it, only asked what I thought of it. Other friends I told showed little interest and I began to feel as though they all saw it as some eccentricity and little more. I can see why Josie hadn't offered it to me earlier. There are meant to be benefits from meditation, all intangible and untraceable. As one might expect from something which relates to traditional sciences only when necessary. I decided to continue, thinking it a small investment. I had the time, especially now that drugs and discos were less a part of my life.

CHAPTER ELEVEN

I was losing touch with everybody that I had partied with. This was a hard time for me because it was when I needed support most and these people were busy carrying on their way and not particularly interested in me if I wasn't. This was clear because they all stopped calling. It was probably best for me. I had to keep a distance for my safety, in case I was persuaded to join them. On questioning how much I cared about these friends, the conclusion I came to was, I don't know. During moments of what felt like strength and enlightenment my conclusion was definite, not at all. This was a murky realisation, because it was like admitting that I had been wrong or at least false, or even conned somehow. No, I'm sure I got a great deal out of my drug-fucked friends and drug-fucked days. Yes I had, at least I had met Marcus and Josie. This was important to me. Marcus could so easily drift out of my life, clearly in that other world and barely in mine. I knew I didn't want this so had to make efforts against it.

I arranged to meet Marcus in the West End, which I increasingly disliked. The bars and cafés reminded me of how many months I had spent using, then less treasured time. After an hour of waiting, I left feeling dejected. I called him, we sorted it out and arranged to meet in the same place. Again he didn't show. I felt so uncomfortable I could have cried. I left and started to walk towards the tube station. Feeling insulted and on a deeper level very lonely a beaming face appeared in front of me.

"Paul, my god you were miles away."

"Trish. No I'm definitely here I'm sorry to say."

"Poor love, having a bad day are we?"

"Yeah. Marcus . . ."

"Say no more."

"We were meant to meet . . ."

"And he didn't show. If I had a dollar for every time . . ."

"A dollar." I burst out laughing. "You're not down under any more Trish, get used to it."

"I'd still rather have dollars, then with all the money I'd have from the Marcus deal, I could get out of this miserable city."

"I know what you mean."

Trish may have known that I needed some company or it may have just been luck that it was convenient for her. Whatever it was, we had a nice day together. I was beginning to wonder if I had any friends at all.

Marcus eventually phoned about a week later. That was after I had left four messages on his answer machine, trying hard not to sound whiny. Instead of arranging to meet yet again, I offered to call round to his flat and pick him up.

It was mid-summer and everything was gorgeous. I had prepared a picnic to take to Hampstead Heath, I needed to lure Marcus out of his den with treats of possible sex. I knew the food wouldn't be enough of an incentive and neither would I. After all we could talk on the phone. As I stepped out of my flat I took a deep breath. My memory rushed ahead of my conscious mind. It took hold and placed me somewhere comfortable, very normal yet still exciting. I caught up with myself and acknowledged a thought, a sense, a smell. It was that of fresh cut grass, sharp and certain. Now in scorching heat, behind classroom glass, a voice, uncaring and dull smears from the teacher's mouth. I'm sleepy and not listening, barely half hearing but quietly longing for it to end. Then this same smell on a wisp of air, cooling, carrying feelings of hope, release from this place stuffed full of tables, oppression and others bored and waiting. So with the breeze comes freedom, at least any time soon, then I would be lying, looking up to the sky, surrounded by buttercup heads. It were as though as I did this, even then I knew how good this was. Why did I let this go?

I couldn't face the tube so caught the bus. It was Sunday so the journey was quite fast. Marcus hadn't got up yet. I expected this so had brought round some fresh coffee which I knew he loved. Marcus answered the door whilst hiding behind it. He was naked and as he ran back to his bed his little bum shook.

"You've had your hair cut."

"Yeah it's my marine look."

As with any image Marcus had, he looked more like a prettified portrait, a touched-up photo with bruised looking lips, perfect skin and the longest lashes. After a quick shower he towel dried his hair, pulled on his jeans, and we were off.

We got a cab to the Heath. Marcus had the money and said that he couldn't stand the journey otherwise. As we walked down the path and into the trees, I couldn't help noticing how well Marcus looked. He was dressed in the most faded denim jeans and jacket which perfectly matched the colour of his eyes.

"Have you been in the sun Marcus?"

"No, I've rented a sunbed. It's great it just slips under the bed, so no one can tell I'm a nelly." I wasn't easily fooled by gay costumes but Marcus looked very sexy. It made me feel like an old fuddy-duddy. I hadn't been to a club in ages and I spent Saturday night preparing a picnic. If I wasn't careful I could end up getting something hideous out of the day.

In the middle of an open space of green we put down the rucksack and laid down our shirts. I didn't bring a blanket, I thought it would be too much. I had also decided not to take all the food out of the bag but just pick things out as we wanted them.

We ate in silence and just as I was going to complain about him not turning up the times before, Marcus said. "Did you hear that?"

"Hear what?"

"That's a robin."

"Where?"

"Hang on, wait till it sings again . . . There, there he is, in the tree there."

On a low branch quite far away was a robin with a red breast.

"Oh yeah."

"It's a fella."

"How did you know it was a robin?"

64

"I used to be into birds when I was a kid. I had books and binoculars, I was even a member of a club."

"I don't believe you."

"Honestly. Promise you won't tell any one though."

"I don't know it depends if you stand me up again." As I said this I wished I hadn't. The whole mood changed.

"You couldn't resist it could you?"

"Well, I waited in that stupid café for an hour."

"Big deal. I was out of my head. The last thing on my mind was meeting for a coffee."

"You make it sound like a crime."

"Get you Miss Prim-and-Proper, like you would have been able to make it six months ago. How quickly things change."

"I'm not going to feel guilty for not doing drugs."

"Fine but don't give me a hard time for doing them."

"I wasn't, I just . . ."

"I don't want to hear it Paul."

There was a nasty atmosphere surrounding us now. The sun was shining and the air was fresh but not where we were sitting. I had so wanted this to be a perfect day, all the ingredients were there. Marcus and I hadn't the same things in common at the moment, that was clear. After a silence I changed the subject by asking about his sex life. Marcus and I had always swapped sex stories but his were always more interesting.

"I made one man pick up another for a three way then got him to pick up another."

"Bossy boots."

"Well I was on coke. Someone's got to organise these things or they never happen."

"That's for sure."

"The four of us played around, making sure that I was the centre of attention with every hole filled.

"It sounds like a circus."

"More like a freak show. I dread to think what any of them looked like."

"Carry on."

"I got bored of two of them, so kept the dirtiest one and

sent the other two home."

"Did they go home together?"

"I don't know. Who cares? Anyway this man ended up putting three apples up my arse."

I burst out laughing. "Were they Cox's?"

"No cooking apples."

"Not even you . . ." We laughed. "What did it feel like?"

"Really comfortable because they weren't going in and out, just sitting there. Meanwhile he could get busy doing other things."

"Jesus Christ!"

"The best thing was when they were up there, I put my finger into my bum and I could touch one of them. The sphincter couldn't close around them."

"Fantastic. Didn't it hurt at all?"

"Probably. I don't know. I was so out of it. Oh yeah . . ." He starts rooting in his jacket pocket. " . . .That reminds me, I brought some acid. Do you want some?"

"You know I don't."

"Go on loosen up a bit."

"No, for God's sake, Marcus."

"I was just asking, don't get annoyed."

"I'm not annoyed, but this is hard enough without my friends insisting. And I'm loose enough." This obviously wasn't true and I resented the accusation.

"You're uptight if you ask me."

"Just because you think everything in life revolves round drugs."

"No. They do make it more interesting though."

"More confused you mean."

"Fuck off Paul, you prick. I suppose you've found Jesus too."

Before the argument could go any further Marcus got up and dusted off.

"I'm going for a walk, see what's here." He then popped the acid into his mouth and started to walk off.

"See you in a minute," I said hopefully.

"If I'm lucky I'll be more than a minute."

Marcus headed towards a clump of trees and I didn't see

him again that day. I lay for a couple of hours, but as the sun started to lose it's heat I headed home. I wasn't sure whether I was angry or sad, and if I was sad, was it for Marcus or myself?

CHAPTER TWELVE

I decided to start back at the gym. This, like many things I did at that time, I did by myself. None of my club friends got up before lunch time and the last thing they would feel like doing is exercising. It was a big deal for me to try this again. I knew that I hated so many things about it and resented so many people who did it. I talked to Gaia about it and got a pep talk off Josie. I even meditated before I went, to try and focus. I was pulling out all the stops. I knew this was going to be difficult.

When I was younger I had started exercising to be healthy. I also realised that I liked the way other boys looked who had good bodies so wanted to be the same. As my own body began to change, I noticed that I was treated differently. I got more attention. It was a particular kind of attention, it was sexual. Enjoying this, I exploited it, had lots of fun and partied hard. As I did, the working out became more difficult. I partied harder and harder as it became more about trying not to notice what I was doing and less about feeling good. Eventually I stopped going to the gym altogether. My self-hatred and sense of failure grew as my body diminished. I started wearing long sleeve shirts which served a duel purpose for they covered the track marks in both of my arms.

Recent history had to be put aside. All my anger towards myself and others had to rest while I effaced the long haul back to where I had once been. The problem was I hadn't liked certain aspects of it the first time. I knew that I didn't understand this completely and even hid from myself the little I did. I felt, though, that I might possibly have more ammunition this time round. I wasn't sure of this, it was only a hunch. Nancy had encouraged me to believe in my intuition and said that if I did it would strengthen.

I went early in the morning on my first day back. I wore a track suit to cover up my body. I was still very pimply and hadn't shaved thinking it hardly worthwhile. The gym was almost empty apart from a couple of familiar faces;

one that acknowledged me as if to say, 'How the mighty have fallen.' Maybe I was just being paranoid but I know how nasty people can be so had to be realistic. I sweated a lot, my eyes looked red and irritated. In short I looked as though I might drop at any second. I obviously had to ease into it slowly. At least I had got this far, I was making a real effort. I had thought it was all down hill and that my health would just deteriorate until I died. I blamed so much on being HIV positive. Here I was, fighting back, thinking I possibly had a future. I began to get a little more excited about life. I had a good reason to get out of bed in the morning and to get into it at night. My sleeping pattern began to normalise due to being so tired from the gym. Again, I had thought that I would never be able to sleep without tablets. I had had so little faith in myself. I had been giving in. I may have even gone along with it if I had continued to IV my drugs. The greatest precaution I ever took was to ask if it was good stuff. I could easily have overdosed and not made it to the hospital. Alternatively I could have vomited and choked in my sleep. It became hard for me to believe that I had so little respect for my life. I guess I thought I was going to die anyway so what the hell.

I told Gaia about my frustration and how angry I got at the gym. It took so long to get a good body and it all seemed pointless anyway.

"Am I doing it for myself or for those men?"

"Who do you think it's for?" Sometimes Gaia was so predictable. I felt I could have stayed at home and just kept throwing questions to and from myself. The funny thing was I did find the process beneficial.

"I want to feel good about myself again."

"This doesn't sound like a problem."

"No I guess it's not but I also want men to be attracted to me."

"Is that a problem?"

"No, well I don't want them just to be attracted to me physically." I was forming the thoughts as I spoke. Often I think I wouldn't have thoughts unless I spoke.

"Why?" she said provoking. "You are attracted to them

69

in that way aren't you?"

"Yes." It wasn't the same though was it? That uncomfortable feeling was there again. I went quiet and stared at her silver shoes. What therapist would wear silver shoes? How distracting. I wondered if she was aware of it. "Do you think about the clothes you wear, do you dress down?" Sometimes I would be allowed to change the subject. She said that if a subject was important enough it would come up again.

"Dressing down, that reminds me of what you told me about your mother dressing up to go to church."

Now she was bugging me. I hadn't wanted to carry on the conversation about the gym but I certainly didn't want to talk about my mother.

"It's almost time." I said as I looked at her watch. I tried not to quote her, for she would always say, 'We're coming to time.'

On the following Tuesday, as she had suggested, I was able to link my session with the previous one. I was still thinking about the gym and I did want to go further with it. So it did carry through. I had needed the weekend to think about it and decided not to fight her, it just wasted our time.

"Maybe I just want to be liked."

"So why do you get angry?"

"Because I know that I'm as superficial as everyone else . . . I don't want to be." How could I expect anyone to treat me any different than I treated them. It was too hideous. In a twisted way it almost seemed just that I should have done this to myself.

This anger didn't go away and it was so self-defeating. I would lose motivation. I couldn't channel energy to lift a weight, it seemed to go inwards and make me weak. Sometimes I wouldn't go at all, not being able to bear the whole process: the paranoia, the anguish, the self-punishment. I did persevere. Maybe it was the catholic in me, torturing myself and assuming that good would come from pain and suffering. I may have even got off on this. How sad I felt at times thinking of the shit my mother put

70

up with. She worked so hard to bring up eight children. Did she enjoy the self-inflicted misery? Some of my saddest memories surround her. Tiny things like getting a new pair of gloves for Christmas and being so pleased. They were mine, not handed down, not shared. They fitted me. They were made for me, bought for me and they were mine. They were grey and woollen and beautiful. On the way to church that day I fell and tore them. The injustice of the world was summed up for me there and then, and still is. Something that seemed so good and lovely was destroyed. I cried so much. Of course my mother sewed them up with PVC patches and she was a saviour, but I can still feel a pang of pain thinking about it.

CHAPTER THIRTEEN

It was early in October and someone had already asked me about possible plans for Christmas. I think this was just in case, as usual, so many people ended up having a miserable time. I hadn't seen Marcus since the picnic. We didn't even speak on the phone at the time. A distance was growing between us because we were not doing the same things anymore. I had started to go to the cinema more, meet friends for coffee and even go to the theatre. Marcus didn't like these things. He found them pretentious. I think he knew that his realm was discos. He felt uncomfortable doing day-time, or more to the point, non-drug oriented things. I knew how he felt for I was still on the edge. If the balance tipped I could be where he was. I felt clumsy and awkward in clubs if I wasn't high and sometimes an idiot socially, just because I was sober. The secret for me was to keep it small, never to meet more than one, at most two, people at a time. I had always to be somewhere where I could talk without shouting. If I had to raise my voice, I felt it had to be to say something worth hearing. I didn't want that pressure. For me clubs were so much about being seen, showing off, pretending to be more than I am, which makes it difficult to say I'm only this. The next step is to be able to say but 'this' has worth, has depth and is interesting. Trying to believe these things, I lived day to day, constantly analysing everything. As always, the more I learnt, the less I felt I knew. I did love Marcus and hoped that there would be a time again soon when we'd spend more time together.

I went to meet Josie for lunch after therapy one Friday. I decided to stop off and get some flowers for Gary who was at the Lighthouse. I heard he was quite sick. I hadn't seen him since last winter. After the last weekend at his flat I thought it best I avoid him. I really didn't know if it was appropriate for me to visit. I always had to go through a little debate in my head when someone I knew was in hospital. Maybe he won't want to see me. Maybe he won't want to see anybody. He may not even want to be seen by anybody. Maybe he's lonely. I usually decided that I would go and see how I was received. I looked around the flower shop. I didn't want anything too bright and cheerful, it seemed too obvious. I knew how snobby people can get about flowers, so no pretty simple ones. I refused to get lilies, thinking they were a cliché of good taste. I saw some others, long hanging purple ones, called 'Love Lies Bleeding.' I loved the name but thought they might be a bit too sombre.

"Having trouble?"

I grunted, barely turning around, thinking I was talking to the shopkeeper. As I acknowledged him I had to do a double take. I wasn't expecting to see what I saw. A man stood obviously trying to catch my eye. He continued, "I'm looking for something for my grandmother."

"Oh." I couldn't help smiling it seemed very obvious that he was trying to make conversation.

"She's had a hysterectomy." Each time he spoke he kind of bent around and under to catch my full attention. I'm surprised I didn't feel embarrassed for he was so attractive, not just his features, although they were a fine balance of the stuff that I dream of, it was his manner so warm with a flicker of a smile on his lips. I felt funny in my stomach but was distracted by his obvious awkwardness.

"Oh," I said again. Now he laughed, realising I was having as much of a problem as he was.

We both stood there. I was transfixed. I could have kissed him there and then.

"I'm going to visit her now." He was doing much better than I was.

"You're so beautiful," I said with a throat full of phlegm. I repeated it as if to make it clearer, but actually it was to acknowledged that I had really said it. He seemed to hang on to the sentence as though his life depended on it. Then he sighed as though something was over, as though we had established everything. I didn't know why I had said it, but I can guess that I had been waiting and holding that sentence for a very long time. It was born of regret and loss and not allowing myself to give up. I had fought with too

73

much for too long not to be able to say: 'You're so beautiful.'
It worked as a force that pulled us together, as though he
knew from my words where I had been and where I so
desperately wanted to go. Again we stood in silence.
"Those are called 'Love Lies Bleeding' your grandmother
might like them," I continued trying to change the subject.

"Hey, back up a little. It's not everyday somebody calls
me beautiful. I noticed you as I was parking and couldn't
believe my luck when you came in here." Could he be
talking about me, have noticed me outside the shop? I
didn't look good and I didn't feel sexy. It was cold, I was so
wrapped up that only a bit of my face was showing. I even
had a cap on. As was my way I couldn't believe what he
had said. I would even have distrusted him but for the way
he expressed himself, so carefully. A careful that comes
from experience not contrived or sly. "Are you very busy?"

"No, I'm never very busy. I'm just going to visit a friend
at the hospital."

"Would you like a lift?"

"It's only a block." I couldn't leave this here, there had to
be more. "Maybe we could meet in the café when you've
finished your visit."

"I'd love to. How long will you be?"

"It's hard to tell I'm not sure what state he is in really."

"Oh, I'm sorry, I hope he's okay."

"Yeah, I'll see soon enough. If I'm going to be a long
time I'll pop down and tell you."

So the arrangement had been made. I bought my flowers,
orange roses, and found Gary asleep. Apparently he was on
Valium and Morphine so there was no point in waiting
around. I wrote him a note and left it on the flowers asking
him to call if he felt up to it. I sat with him a few minutes.
He was wasting and only vaguely looked like the man I
knew. I couldn't help thinking about how people came in
and out of my life. I got hold of his hand, it was so frail. I
left the ward feeling conscious of how I was meant to be
behaving and even how I should be responding. As often
my self-consciousness out-weighed my original feelings.

When I was alone in bed that night, I tried to think what

impact visiting Gary might have had on me. Again I was distracted by the acknowledgement that I was having to think about it in that way to begin with.

When I arrived at the café my man was already there. I must have been longer than I thought.

"How is he?" I shrugged in response and was already thinking that my date was even more handsome than I remembered.

"Let me just get a bottle of water." My lips were suddenly very dry. "Would you like anything?"

"Yes, your name."

"Oh sorry, it's Paul." I was at least sure of that. "And you?"

"Rick. Rick Cochrane." It always seemed to add an air of self-confidence when people introduced themselves with their surname. It took me by surprise. I thought maybe it was unnecessary but remembered that Americans did seem to have a tendency to do this. Whatever. I thought I would allow him to get away with it. At least it wasn't confused or insecure.

While I was at the counter getting served, I thought I'd catch another look at him, just to see what he looked like from a distance. He was watching me and was going to look away, but smiled. It seemed like I could feel that smile deep inside my belly and it fed something. I knew on my return to the table I would have to fake being comfortable and charming. Maybe not. Why should I be taken seriously? What had I to offer?

"So Mister Cochrane." I just couldn't resist it. "That sounds very adult. Are you a school teacher?"

"No, just a bit officious." He responded very well and looked as though he could have dealt with anything I threw at him.

"How is he?" he reminded me.

"He was asleep." Feeling my way, I went a little further. "I could hardly recognise him. He's lost so much weight." Rick looked down at his coffee, then returned a look into my eyes, not aggressive but very definite. "Are you close to him?"

"Close enough to hate it all."

75

"Always close enough to hate it all." This man really seemed to know what I was talking about.

Our conversation had already broken rules. To talk about something we cared about was not usual. Although it was becoming more acceptable as everyone was having to face these things everyday.

"He has pneumonia, who knows?"

"Listen, this is just a guess but I think you could do with someone being really nice to you. What do you say?"

"Sounds about right to me. Do you know anyone?"

"Yes I do and he'd like to take you out for dinner tonight. If you're not busy."

" Let me think." I waited a few seconds with a look of concentration on my face. "I think I'm free. Yes I'm almost sure of it. Is this friend of yours okay though?"

"You'll have to see for yourself. I think he'd like you though. He's a friend of my grandmother." I couldn't help laughing. I felt comfortable playing in this way and he responded so well. It was set and I couldn't wait.

I was able to have sex with Rick for about three weeks. I liked this and thought it very healthy. Then for some reason it took a turn. I started to feel uncomfortable even kissing him, so I stopped. I thought this fickle at first, but decided that it was the right thing to do. Why should I do anything that doesn't feel right just because I'm meant to. It was too late in my life to try and start following a norm, just for the sake of it. I spoke to Gaia. The most obvious explanation was that, as I was getting closer to Rick, I found it more difficult to connect the sex and emotion. I wondered at first if I just didn't find him sexy. I had been wary of getting too familiar with him physically, in case I found a flaw. So in a Victorian kind of way, I had only fucked him without really exploring the ins and outs of his body. I didn't actually know how big his dick was. It was as though I was afraid to face it. I hated this idea, again it seemed so superficial or just fucked up.

Gaia asked me about having sex with punters. Did I get a hard on? Yes. Did I find them repulsive? To a certain extent yes, but this didn't mean that I couldn't be turned on by, or have sex with, them. So it would follow that if I no longer found Rick sexy, I would still be able to have sex with him. But I didn't, so it must have been a choice, and not necessarily of my mind.

I pointed out to Gaia that it was becoming clear that sex without emotion was unsatisfying, yet sex with emotion was still unattainable. This was something that ran deep inside. Knowing it was there was a little of the battle. All I had to do then was find out what the barrier was all about. I began to feel less guilty about what was happening between Rick and I. It felt like a fork in a road with a block at each entrance. I could no longer indulge myself in exploring the world of creative sex for it's own sake. Yet I was a child unable to even enter the world of connected sex and emotion, unprepared for what love might be.

CHAPTER FOURTEEN

November came quickly, I had been so wrapped up with Rick. My sister had left a message on my machine so I felt I had to get back to her. Whenever this happened I always dreaded my mother answering and would often put off phoning all together.

"Hello it's Paul. Who's that?"

"Hello, it's mum here." I always thought it funny that she called herself mum.

"Hi, how are you?"

"Alright."

"How's dad?" She must have known I was being false now.

"Fine. What have you been up to?"

"You don't want to know what I've really been doing." I was probing just to see.

"Well I don't want to hear the gory details, but I'd like to know how you feel." I was surprised by her response, it did seem realistic to me. I wouldn't want to hear the gory details either.

"There aren't that many gory details at the moment." I lightened on this remembering that my life had changed quite a lot since I last spoke to her. Also she did seem different. It had been about six years.

"I'm sure there are." She laughed. It was good to hear. I felt a bit mixed up.

"Well, maybe. No, but seriously, things have changed quite a lot for me."

"What do you mean? In what way?" This was the first time I had to think back in this way, to make a simple list. For some reason I didn't really want to. I suddenly felt as though I had to justify myself.

"Nothing really, I'm just not as mad as I was."

"How's your health?" Oh, no. Why so soon?

"Do you really want to know? I'm not prepared to lie anymore, not for anyone."

"Don't worry, Pauly, I know all about it, Helen told me."

I froze. She already knew. I suddenly felt as though I had a sense of her pain and her strength. What must it have taken to be able to say that to her son, more to the point, to have held on to that knowledge and not been able to speak to me. Had I been so cruel? "Pauly, I just want to be a part of your life again. I know I was stupid. I felt as though I was loosing you. I couldn't bear to think what you got up to. I just didn't want any harm to come to you . . . For some reason it all came out as anger. The last thing in the world I wanted was to drive you away . . . Then whatever I tried to say to fix it, came out wrong and drove you further away." I tried to speak but couldn't, crying noises were all that would have come out. "Pauly?"

". . .Yeah?"

"I love you."

I was speechless. She had said so much. I still felt unsure, it were as though I wasn't prepared to give in that easy. It had gone on too long to be resolved in one little phone call. "Pauly?"

My name grated. I heard her voice and it was desperate and wounded. It was not how I ever wanted my name to sound.

"Pauly?"

"Can I call back? I have to think," I said slowly, my words broken, my breathing irregular.

This was on a Thursday. I tried to remember everything that had been said, so that on the following morning I knew exactly where I wanted to begin.

"I want to talk about my mum. I spoke to her last night."

"How was that?" said Gaia as she rested her head at a slight angle, so that one of her ears was further forward than the other. This meant she was ready to listen. I had seen people do this in railway stations when announcements were made over the tannoy. I usually thought it affected but in this context it seemed a part of her job, to act, so I didn't mind. I saw it merely as a language, no more false than saying that she was listening.

"I phoned to speak to my sister. I didn't expect to have to deal with my mum."

"What do you mean deal with?"

"Well somehow the conversation slid off the path and then we were in the middle of talking about the argument. She knew that I was positive, Helen had told her." I paused too long.

"How did you feel about Helen telling her?"

"I was a bit shocked, she just came out with it. She said she knew all about it and that she had been angry, but that it was just that parts of my life were hard to accept. She sounded upset. She said she . . ."

I couldn't finish the sentence. I couldn't say 'she loved me'. Gaia passed me the box of tissues and I laughed. "She said she . . ."

It happened again. I gave up. Gaia waited a while until I had stopped blowing my nose and sniffling. I couldn't look up at her. I never could when I cried. I wouldn't like to feel as though I was exploiting my tears as if to say, 'Look at me showing all this emotion.' I guess there's no need to look at her, it was about me after all. "The funny thing is I don't feel like it's sorted out. I don't think I want it to just be forgiven. There's something else too. I can't piece it together properly but it's something like: If everything is resolved then my life is over. If I don't have this problem there's no need to carry on. I don't understand it any more than that but I definitely feel something along those lines."

Gaia looked puzzled. I tried to explain further but ended up just saying the same thing using different words. We sat in silence for a while, presumably both wondering what this could possibly mean. That was how we worked by that point. I would often suggest things to her and she would sometimes develop them or let them go. Eventually she took her fingers away from her lips to speak.

"I'm not sure but I'm thinking along the lines of identity."

I hadn't a clue what she was talking about so had to wait for more. "Something to do with you creating an identity as an individual that she was not a part of. Perhaps you might feel as though you would be losing your identity, your life, if she accepts your life. I don't know, I think it's probably more complicated than that as well. This is something I'm sure we'll come back to."

What Gaia had said left my mind spinning. Confused, but somehow reassured, I left. We had come to time.

I received a letter from Loz, it read.

Dearest Paul,

I will be in London next Thursday. I would love to see you. I will be in Westminster Cathedral at ten o'clock.

Loz.

It was rare that Loz came to London. There was a time when she would visit Sister Thérèse but now it was only ever for a specific art exhibition. I was excited at the prospect of seeing her and prepared myself with things I wanted to talk about and questions I wanted to ask. I woke that morning to the purest of November days. Winter was being held off for now and the sharp sunlight caught every shape. It gave well defined angles to buildings and gilded the smallest of twigs. These days seemed so special for they were here for such a short time. I tried to respect this and used them well. I walked all the way from Earl's Court to Victoria. I even went the long way round via Hyde Park. It took me over an hour in all but I wasn't going to miss a second of this day. I set off at eight o'clock, planning to stop for breakfast on the way, so I arrived at Westminster Cathedral at about nine-thirty.

As I entered, again, as always I was stunned into silence and reverence. The affect it has is not intentional. The original design is incomplete, but what has been created is so much more. The unfinished ceiling creates a depth which provokes the internal. Something of heaven has been created. I entered feeling prepared for this, but I obviously wasn't. Thoughts of my childhood came rushing back to me, of confession and Stations of the Cross. My mother and I sat close together in a cold, near empty church. This was something we shared, no one else in the family ever went

81

to extra services, because they didn't have to. This was exactly why I liked it, for I had chosen to go. I knelt to pray and I felt very holy. I loved this time for I believed it all. God was there with me, watching and listening. He would make sure no harm came to me or my mother. God knew everything that I thought and felt, He knew I was good.

I felt sad that this was gone: no more faith in ultimate good, in something that cared beyond all else. Surely this was all I ever wanted since those evenings, from something or someone.

I was sure that I was being watched. The whore walking up the centre of the aisle. Shouldn't I have come in through the back door and begged entrance from people who were better than me. I went right up to the altar, feeling a certain strength that this was where I had come from. I was allowed to face this God because He at least knew me and must remember my naive love. I stood and gazed into the pit above me, then feeling self-conscious, I sat down. I chose the front row so that I could easily be found, but right to the side so as not to spoil the view for anyone else. The light drew away quickly from the centre aisle, so I knelt in a half-light. I closed my eyes. This was familiar, the smells and the softened noises. I thought of Kevin.

'Lets talk,' he had said but I didn't get the chance. I felt less angry at him than I had and thought of the the way he laughed. It used to feel so good making him laugh like that.

I opened my eyes. If I didn't look behind me everything was still and peaceful. I looked at my watch. It was still only nine-forty. I had twenty minutes to wait. I decided to meditate. Again I closed my eyes. I breathed deeply in preparation. I went in to it smoothly and quickly with no physical distractions like twitching or scratching. I silently murmured my mantra. There were gaps of time where I was aware of nothing, then softly eased in a notion of Josie, her smile and her first hello.

"I must remember to call Marcus" I said inside my head. "Keep to my mantra." I reminded myself, so I did.

I felt someone kneel down beside me. I opened my eyes and there was Loz. I looked at my watch, it was ten already.

82

"Loz."

"I didn't want to disturb you, I thought you might be praying," she whispered giggling.

"Hardly," I said, faking a big frown whilst trying to keep my voice down.

"I saw you from way off and I thought my little boy is kneeling praying to Jesus for being so bad."

I loved the way she teased me like that, the running joke being that I was her boy. As we spoke I slowly came round more from where I had been. Sometimes it took a while. I felt calm and very nice being with Loz.

"I want to light candles at the back. Are you finished? What were you doing? Were you praying?"

"No. I was meditating."

"What! You've started meditating? When? Why? Tell me all about it?"

"Well let's go and sort out the candles first."

At the back Loz took out some change from her pocket to put in the charity box.

"It's well worth it," she said with a wink. She lit three candles.

"Why three?" I said.

"Sssh. One's for my sweetheart Mary, one's for Saint Thérèse and one's for my *Ange du peche*. Do you know what that means?" She grinned.

"Angel of something?"

"Good boy. My angel of sin. You my little Paul."

Loz was so sweet to me, she made me believe that she cared.

We linked our arms as we walked down the steps at the entrance. We went to a café and talked for some time. I told her about how and why I began to meditate. This led on to Josie, then how I was spending my time, then on to Rick, then I skated over sex and straight on to therapy. I gave a synopsis of what I thought I knew. I'm sure Loz made up a picture of her own, interpreting what I had said. I walked her back to Victoria station and as we parted she squeezed my hand.

"You're not sweating," she said.

"Why should I be nervous?" I said being cocky.

"Come visit sometime and bring Rick if you like, he sounds lovely."

"He is."

Loz got on her train and went back to Brighton. When I got home that day there was a message on the answer phone from my mother. It was rare to have so much worth remembering in one day. The message asked plainly if I would like to go home for Christmas that year. I hadn't done this for ages. I had trouble with the idea. Firstly I had friends who were closer than most of my family. I usually spent it with others who were waiting for it all to be over. Secondly there seemed to be so much falseness surrounding Christmas and the last thing my mother and I needed was this. It was a picture of hell to my mind and I didn't want to be a part of it. I made up my mind and called her back.

"Hello, mum?"

"Hello, Pauly." She sounded so happy to hear me.

"It's about coming up there, I'd like to see you, but I can't bear all that Christmas stuff. I don't fit in. I've got nothing in common with anyone anymore." She was silent. "I would like to see you, honestly, but I want to be with my friends and Rick, my boyfriend."

"Why don't you come up the week before. There will be no fuss. No one else will be around apart from your dad and me." I had no choice. It did seem like a good idea.

"Alright," I said slowly, slightly surprised that the idea didn't sound so bad. It was agreed, and anyway it was sometime off yet. I spoke to Rick about it all and he was fantastic, as he was proving always to be. He even asked if I would like him to pick me up when I was ready to come home. He suggested that it was probably best that I went up by myself so that my mum and I could have some time alone. He said that he would love to meet her and thought nothing of driving a hundred miles to rescue me. He was so cute and so thoughtful. I agreed, thinking I would much rather have him to look at all the way home than the bleak winter landscape from a train window. I was only going for a weekend but it took a lot of effort mentally. My planned visit was the topic of conversation during most of my following sessions with Gaia. Although it became clear that we couldn't go any further until after I got back.

I got a postcard from Loz about a week after I had seen her.

Dear Paul,

It seemed so right to talk to you again. It's as if something we both had to work out has been worked out in our different ways.

Remaining yours Loz.

It did seem as though something had been worked out between us. I knew that I had been somewhere and that I had come nearer to Loz again and nearer to myself.

CHAPTER FIFTEEN

I got a phone call from Marcus's brother, Donald. I didn't know him. I had never heard of him before. Marcus had asked him to call me to tell me that he was in hospital. When hearing this I remember being more shocked than upset. I also had a self-centred feeling of 'it's getting closer'. 'It' being illness and death. I knew that Marcus had been positive for eight or nine years now. I also knew that he had the most unhealthy lifestyle of anyone I could think of. He seemed to use up all of his resources all of the time but still he was always so strong. Of course I went through all the usual thoughts about my feelings and constructing ideas of how I should respond and behave. I then deconstructed all this in search of some kind of truth about how I felt. It still all seemed more about me.

"Just go and see how he is," I said.

"What's the point?" I replied.

"Because he might want to see you. He might need you. He might feel scared."

"What can I do to help?"

"Just be there. At worst you'll be a distraction."

"I know this scenario already. Why go through it again?"

"Because this time it's Marcus."

Marcus. I couldn't bear to think of him unhappy or sick. I didn't get flowers, it seemed too silly. This was real life and all that was really needed was to get to him, and then take it from there.

On that Monday morning London had never seemed so grim. The traffic was heavy, the tube unbearable and nobody seemed to care what I was feeling. It was drizzling, not cleaning, just wetting and dragging down all the filth that sat in the sky. I was sticky and felt grubby. What the hell am I doing living here? Why do I put up with this shit? Thoughts like these were barely intense enough to outweigh the despair in my mind already.

As I approached Marcus's bed I saw that he was sleeping. He had tubes coming out from his body with some breathing apparatus next to his mouth. That can't be him I thought. Marcus was different than that, he was tough and vital. I walked back out into the corridor and began to cry.

I found my way to the canteen and had to wait about three quarters of an hour until I was ready again. I knew then that a lot of my emotion was self-pitying but I knew also that it had to be dealt with, or at least looked at.

I approached Marcus's bed again. He was lying very still with his head turned towards a window. I went around to be in his field of vision. His eyes were open yet he didn't seem to be awake. Then slowly he began to move his head as though he were only becoming aware that there was someone beside him.

"Paul," he said so softly. His lips were dry with white saliva frosting the edges. I bent over and kissed him. I made some space on the bed and hugged him. I felt a rush of emotion, and had to think of the most ridiculous things I could to stop myself crying. "It looks so beautiful out," he continued and seemed slightly lost in his own thoughts. "More seems to happen in winter."

I was used to the way Marcus spoke. He was very romantic at times. I used to joke saying that it had something to do with the amount of drugs we took. He would answer that it was the reason we took so many drugs. Looking out of the window he said. "You look great."

I wasn't going to let him get away with being so cheeky. "Yeah you too."

"You bastard," he said slowly and rolled his eyes as if to say how could you. I was relieved. Marcus was still very much alive. I had been frightened that he would know what was going on. I had thought of every possible horror that I could have from the time Donald had phoned.

"How long have you been here?" Then not waiting for an answer "I wish you had got hold of me earlier."

"There wasn't time, it all happened so quickly. There was so much shit to deal with. I didn't expect all this now."

"How do you feel?"

"Top of the world."

His spirits seemed high enough considering, but there

was something else about him, a depth or a heaviness. Maybe it was just a resignation.

"Really, how do you feel?"

"I don't know, confused."

"Do you know what's happening? When will you be getting out?"

"They're doing some x-rays of my chest."

"Is there anything you want?"

"Yeah, there is, but I can't ask you yet, not till I know more."

"Marcus, tell me what is it? I can always get it now just so you'll have it."

"No, it's not like that. I'll tell you later."

"But . . ."

"Let it rest, Paul. How's things with you and Rick?"

"Alright, well as alright as it gets for me. We're not having sex. I do like him a lot but I don't know if there's any future in it. I thought he was sure about it all, that was part of the reason I liked him so much. I thought maybe things would sort themselves out."

"What do you want out of it?"

"I don't know, a boyfriend?"

"Come on, you know better than that."

"I don't know better. The thing is I know he's becoming less sure of us. I don't know if it's impatience or just that he realises that it's never going to be, you know, normal. I'm a prostitute. He says he doesn't mind but it's not about him, it's about me. I know it affects me and I don't even know if stopping will help."

"And you're not prepared to try."

"Something like that. Well, not until I feel like it. I'm hoping that I'll feel like it one day."

"If anyone is capable of sorting it all out, you are."

"Marcus, that's really sweet but I wish I believed it. I do have some faith. Oh, I don't know."

"Well I'm glad you came to tell me your problems. I haven't a care in the world."

"I'm sorry, Marcus. I'm a selfish bugger. How long have you been here?"

"About three weeks."

"Jesus. I wish I knew earlier."

"It's good to see you now anyway."

"Does anybody else know you're here? Has anyone been in?"

"It's funny, you know. I couldn't really think of anyone else I wanted to tell. I don't really feel like seeing anyone. It's not exactly social. What's even funnier is that I wanted to see my brother, of all people. I haven't seen him in years."

"What about your mum and dad?"

"Don said that mum wants to come. She's going to try and make it as soon as she can."

"Do you want me to tell anyone how they can get hold of you?"

"Like who?"

Marcus looked at me so sincerely and I only then realised exactly what he was saying. There was no one else, no one he wanted to see. What the hell was it all about? When it came to it, so many of the people we spent time with didn't matter. This was depressing, in that I felt so hopeless, but I wouldn't let it out, not then, not with Marcus, although it made me think again about everyone around me.

CHAPTER SIXTEEN

It was the beginning of December, the city centre was full of decorations and people busy shopping. This made me want to get out of town so I asked Rick if we could go for a drive into the country. I had in the back of my mind stuff that needed sorting out between him and me, so this seemed a good opportunity. It was a Saturday, so Rick was off work. The weekend seemed to mean more to him because he had a regular job. We set off in the afternoon and headed out towards Windsor. We drove around country lanes and walked along the side of the Thames. We had lunch at some horrid restaurant, one of a chain, styled like an old fashioned inn. We drove some more, then eventually stopped again beside a field. It was simple, flat and green. It was an ideal spot to view the sunset. We got out of the car and sat against the bonnet which was warm. The air was getting cooler. I thought of the contrast between the car and the field, the artificial and the natural. Then I changed my mind, it was the car that was real and something about the field was unreal. It seemed as though something was instigating these ideas or feelings. The strangest thing about this was that this something seemed to have a presence. I almost felt I was seeing this. Perhaps I was? What I was seeing was the field. It struck me that I had had this experience before. A couple of weeks earlier I had been in my flat and was taking a bath. I heard a noise and got spooked by it. I let it get to me so much that I had to check all the windows to make sure they were closed and then double lock the front door. I spoke to Gaia about it. I told her that I didn't believe in spirits and wouldn't until I had had first hand experience. This was reassuring enough, except it was possible that the first hand experience could happen at any time. I sat in my bathtub feeling scared. I tried to think logically and rationalise about the situation.

I had clearly been opening myself up over the last year to accepting a more emotional and even a more spiritual side of life. Yet, because it was all still very unclear, I was probably confusing everything intangible. Then I was lumping it altogether and labelling it 'spirit.'

"I think there probably is confusion. I think your fear has more to do with your own aggression. As with the s&m, you know what there is to be scared of, because you have it within yourself. You heard a noise and you read it as an aggressor."

Gaia's suggestion had seemed to make sense to me then, so why shouldn't I apply it to other situations? What was I giving off to feel such a presence in the field? I didn't know because I wasn't sure what the presence felt like to begin with. I did know that it didn't scare me.

I asked Rick if he minded if I meditated.

"It will only take twenty minutes." I said apologetically.

"I'll wait in the car." he said. Then as he looked at me, a thought appeared to click in his head. "Oh sorry, what am I saying? I'll sit here with you."

I burst out laughing. He was trying very hard to be understanding and realised that it might be nicer if we shared the moment. We sat close on the car. I closed my eyes and breathed deeply. I could smell the earth and feel the damp. I thought through images of peeling back and entering into something within my mind. This was one process I used as preparation before drifting into meditation. Every now and then I would return to notice my senses responding to my environment, the field, then leave all this again. A thought of the conversation I was intending to have with Rick drifted into my mind. It seemed clear and simple with a direction and a goal. I let this idea go, feeling confident of it, and continued to drift.

"Twenty minutes have gone."

I had asked Rick to tell me when the time was up. I found this more comforting than an alarm which some people used. Most times I would just guess, then when checking if there was still time left I simply closed my eyes and carried on. Sometimes I would be gone for forty minutes before thinking to check the time. Nancy had told me to stick to the twenty minutes for it was a safety valve to only deal with so much at a time. If someone was with me,

91

on the other hand, I was allowed to go longer. Apparently Nancy used to meditate for hours when in India with the Maharishi.

"Thanks, Rick."

I put my arm around him and pulled him closer to me. We hugged. I could smell his breath, the wax on his skin, the grease in his hair. I started to get a hard on. I pictured him naked. Sections of his body flashed into my mind, disembodied and abstract but not enough to not form a response which was by now very familiar. I felt repulsed by Rick, sexually. I began: "When I'm with you and I hold you I love how affectionate I feel."

"My god, where's this leading? As if I can't tell."

"Please let me finish. I feel very close to you but there is this block when I think about sex." I watched him as I know Gaia watches me.

"Go on. What do you mean by block?"

"When the idea of sex comes into my head, it makes me cringe."

I took a pause again to see how he was responding. "It's almost like the idea of having sex with my mum or dad. This feeling just says no."

Rick burst out laughing.

"It makes you cringe, that's nice." I don't know whether he was nervous, covering his embarrassment or just found it very ridiculous, but something did break.

"I can't help it. It's not what I want, believe me. I've never felt more sure of anyone. I know I can trust you which is so important for me, but there is this feeling and I can't get over it just yet. I was hoping that therapy would help, and I know I can't change over-night, but this isn't good for either of us. I don't want to keep you hanging on for ever with no promise of change. This in turn puts pressure on me. I'm getting all screwed up about it."

This conversation turned into a speech winding round and about, but what was eventually decided was that Rick should look for sex elsewhere. Meanwhile I had to take my feelings of failure and try to look positively at it all. Josie said that just because it didn't work with Rick, doesn't mean I wasn't capable of a love and sex relationship. Gaia suggested that I was probably trying to piece the relationship together artificially. I tried to make it work because I thought that Rick was suitable. Maybe there will be someone one day with whom I will continue wanting to have sex with. But until then I shouldn't force it and confuse myself.

If only I could have chosen how I felt about people during my life then I would have chosen to have a love affair with Rick, have sex and love him. If I could have chosen, he would have been at the top of the list. If life were that simple. Some people might ask: would you have chosen to love someone like Marcus, who you knew was HIV positive, and who lived life precariously as a norm? I would say that I would never invite pain into my life, unless that is, I thought it was worth it. Marcus was definitely worth it.

Sunday afternoon I went back to the hospital to see Marcus. I hadn't spoken to him on the Saturday. He said that this was what he wanted. I think he hadn't wanted to take up all my time. I wasn't going out at night at that time. Rick had decided to spend less time with me to get his head together. Therapy took up two mornings a week, the gym three, so I had two mornings and every afternoon for Marcus. The evenings I tried to keep free to make money, which meant doing a couple of punters a week, although having to be there to receive phone calls was a full time job. On the whole I had plenty of time for him and ultimately he was a priority.

I decided to decorate my flat. I always thought that if I did it, I would like to spend a lot of time on it, so I hadn't ever bothered. I decided to try and create something sombre. I had an idea of old people, plants, table cloths and a loud ticking clock. I had been slowly collecting stuff over the years, including a picture of the Passion which my mother had given me when I left home. This depicted scenes beginning with Judas the traitor all the way through to the Ascension. It was stained, the glass had smashed long ago, but it reminded me of the good things about religion.

I had a conversation with Marcus on the Tuesday which

93

I thought seemed to be heading the opposite way from me. He explained, "When I was at home, I would lie in bed looking at the wall. I did it all the time. There's a dirty mark where a picture was. I had stared at this same spot so often that I could still imagine the picture in detail. There are dirty marks like this all over my bedroom. When my room mate left . . . I asked him to leave . . . he took his pictures with him, but I can still see them. So I don't see the need to have such things around me anymore."

"But they're not just for you, are they? Your room and the things in it are about expressing 'you.' The idea is that you are reassured by it and others understand you by it."

"I don't invite anyone into my room anymore so that's not an issue, and as far as being reassured by it, I'm reassured that it isn't important to me any more. It's all about deconstruction," he said precisely. He had obviously thought about this already.

"In what sense?"

"It's about getting rid of things that aren't necessary in life. It's why some people say I'm so vile. I'm not nice to people anymore."

"But it's not necessary to be vile either."

"It's not that I am vile, I've just got rid of the faking, the pretending. It takes energy to be nice or vile, but it takes nothing to be nothing. It's the same with furniture, friends, clothes, hair-dos, you name it. It seems apt that I end up here with nothing familiar around me. My friends have become fewer and fewer until there's only a couple left. Ultimately I die by myself. It ends up, being about shitting and eating, hot and cold. It's all very basic, just like a baby. I imagine that even love in the end is more about who's looking after me, helping me function."

"That sounds bleak."

"It sounds realistic to me."

"So you end up a hermit in a cave on a mountain."

"No, because comfort is still necessary. Not big velvet sofas, but duvets and beds and warmth are essential."

"So there you are being kept clean, warm and alive."

"Yes, but the being alive can become less of a comfort

too."

"I see. I know what you mean."

Then Marcus's tone changed from matter of fact, to matter of fact with that sincerity that he had shown last time I saw him.

"There's more. This is something very important to me, you can't let me down."

"I won't, well I'm almost sure of it, well, I guess it depends on what it is."

"Paul, the way my life is at the moment isn't much fun. You can see me, I don't look well. Luckily my mind is still here. It's the only thing I ever liked about myself. If I lost it . . . well lets just say I'd hate that. I'd hate to be that mad man over in bed number three who causes problems from early in the morning. You wouldn't like to see this. I wouldn't like to see this, but this isn't what I wanted to say. It's only going to get worse . . ."

I started to cry, and it was on the hill-side. I was half looking up as I saw how sad it was to hear someone I loved say these things to me. I was half looking down as I saw how sure he was to talk in this way and how much love was between us.

"Don't cry, Paul . . . You're so sweet."

I sat in silence. I stared out of the window. I couldn't look at him. "Paul you have to be really strong, I need this from you. I'm scared. I don't know how much pain I'm going to have to deal with and I'm scared because I didn't plan this and I don't know what happens next, but this can't go on."

"What do you mean?"

"There's going to be a time soon when I'll want to stop all this shit."

"What are you saying?"

"You know what I'm saying. There's a few things I want to do. Letters I want to write, people I want to see, mainly my family."

"Marcus?"

"Paul, come on."

I wouldn't acknowledge what he wanted, not then,

although it was all I thought about for the next few days. I found lots of excuses for not visiting him after that. I knew that I was going up to the Lake District to see my mum on the weekend, so I called in on the Thursday night before. Marcus seemed to have deteriorated so much, could it have been true? I felt so annoyed that I hadn't been in earlier.

"How do you feel?"

"Top of the world."

Marcus seemed more down than the last time I had seen him. I thought maybe he was pissed off. It turned out that he was actually in more pain. As with everything in life, I had assumed it had something to do with me. "I feel so uncomfortable all the time."

"What is it, what's uncomfortable?"

"Everything. Oh I don't know. I can't tell. I'm taking pain killers but it all feels so numb and . . ."

"And what?"

"And so pointless."

I had no answer for this. I couldn't see the point of life at the best of times, so hadn't a clue in this case.

"Has your mother been in?"

"No, not yet."

"Do you know when she's coming?"

"I haven't heard yet." I felt a twist of my heart as I realised what might be going on. Maybe she didn't want to see him. "She's very busy. My sister's gone on some course with work and had to leave her kids with mum."

I didn't dare push it any further. I couldn't bear to imagine what his mother might be thinking and how pain-ful that might be to Marcus. How alone was he? Apart from Donald no one in his family had visited him. He told me that he wasn't too bothered about seeing most of them but he was looking forward to seeing his mum.

"You remember that I'm going home, just for the weekend. I'll be back on Monday. I want to get it over with before Christmas." I felt I was having to pretend to be against things we weren't meant to believe in. I felt false and awkward. Was this to be the beginning of lies I thought I'd have to tell Marcus to protect him. What from? Why

96

should anybody ever be protected from the truth? I got ready to go.

"Paul, will you think about what I asked you on Monday?" He caught me off guard and I wasn't able to create more falseness.

"Marcus you know I'd do anything for you." His reply was a smile. It was so deeply confusing to see a smile meaning something which seemed so wrong. Deeper, this smile was based on a love that shows itself at times. It cancels everything else out, fear, selfishness, rules and laws. I understood what he wanted and I knew I would try to be there for him, whatever it took.

"See you Monday then. Thanks, Paul. I quite like you."

"Ninny! See you on Monday. I'll call you from my mum's."

I left feeling as though I were still sitting there, still in a moment of hatred of everything that had ever caused pain. I kept carrying this moment, it became just another part of my life, another part of me.

At the weekend I took the train up to Preston, then another on to where my mum lived. I read some of the way and slept the rest. In between were the usual distractions of other people making noise and just being there. I hated the journey and felt like I was wasting my time or somehow going backwards, back to my family, the house where I lived and all the things I left home to avoid. It didn't seem to make sense, but so little did.

The front of the house looked much the same. The door was open as usual. I went inside, ringing the door bell as I closed it behind me. My mother came out of the kitchen, she had been cooking. She began nervously: "I'm in the middle of making you some apple crumble."

"I love your crumble."

"I know you do, it's for you. There's no one else here but dad."

"Where is he?"

"He had a meeting down at the church for a fund-raiser they're doing. He'll probably go for a drink with the other men afterwards. He shouldn't be back till late."

So it was just me and her. She was much older, but because she looked so familiar, I couldn't tell how she had aged. I could still see her as I've seen her ever since I was a boy, but also I saw a woman who was frail, who had problems, who lived in the same nasty world as I did. When she smiled, I felt she knew the same joys and the same love. I thought all this as I watched her talk and as I answered, but really I was somewhere else. I was still with Marcus, still with Gaia, still with Rick. I was with all these people or rather they were all with me. In fact they were me. I was simply sitting there with my mother and we were talking to each other. It felt nice. We did the things she always did. We drank lots of tea. She showed me clothes she had made, which I know she didn't do with my other brothers. I was asked about my friends and what I was doing, but not in too much detail. I got shown around the garden. Then as it got dark her day was ending. We sat down in the living room and the television went on. When I lived at home, I would always find things to do: drawing, painting, anything but watch t.v. It always irritated me. It wasn't about my inner world, my desires or my beliefs. I knew that there were good programmes on, but there was so much rubbish in between. I never found it relaxing watching people try to sell me things. My mother seemed to enjoy this, so I wanted to do it with her. She sat in her corner of the settee where everything was at hand: her sewing basket, reading lamp, and table for her coffee. I sat too.

The room was decorated for Christmas. I recognised some of the ornaments on the tree. So many familiar but strange things. The strangest of all was the mantelpiece covered with photographs of weddings, babies and cousins. I didn't understand what it was all about. It meant nothing to me. They weren't about friendship, something we earn. I didn't get the connection between all these strangers. Thoughts like these whirled through my head as I sank further into the settee. My mother offered me biscuits. The heat of the room and the blur of t.v made me switch off to what was around me. All I knew was that I was safe and warm and my mother was kind. She wanted

so badly for me to be happy, more importantly to be happy
with me in her life, and I felt like I was. As much of her life
as I could be apart of, I was happy to be there. I could taste
biscuit in my mouth, and hear the blur, and vaguely see the
white lights on the Christmas tree. I thought of New York
from high above, of Gregory, and of Central Park. I must
have leaned on to my mum because I could smell her
perfume. It never smelt like anything in particular, just
perfume. A scent that used to drench her coat when I was
tiny, it would engulf me to keep me warm on cold mornings
in church. The smell always made me a little sick, but I
found it comforting all the same. Then I could feel the soft
wool of her cardigan and her warmth against my face. She
breathed in and out. I don't know how long this lasted.
How many downers had I taken, trying to recreate this?
The security of sleep.

I woke up with a blanket over me. It was quiet. My
mother had gone to bed but the lights on the tree still shone.
They made me feel so much. The glimmerings specks
seemed to contain so many strong memories. It was
Christmas, but not the one that I had been brought up with.
It was just another day when I was reminded of how it's
meant to be and how far from it we were. I fell asleep again.

CHAPTER SEVENTEEN

Now that Rick and I were not seeing each other, I thought it best that I caught the train back to London. The landscape was bleak but at least I felt I had achieved something with my mother. It seemed artificial, a construction to bridge a gap, but what is communication if not only ever this. It's very rare that it's more pure. At least we had something. We knew we loved each other in some way, that was the important thing. The funny thing was, trying to talk made it seem like we didn't. My mother isn't a person I would call if I had a problem. I wouldn't ask for her advice. What was she for then? Of all the interesting relationships in my life that could be developed, why did I waste time with her? Why was she so deep inside me?

I went straight to the hospital. Marcus was sitting listening to a Walkman cassette player. I told him about the last two days, making sure I played it down to just the events. I didn't want to explain what I thought I had got out of it. He listened, then joked.

"You make the train journey sound more interesting than seeing your mum."

"It doesn't sound like it means much but it doesn't take much from her to have an affect."

"I know."

I stroked his head. He closed his eyes and purred. At this we laughed and straight out of this he said: "There's a book. I don't know where you can get it. It tells you about suicide."

My laughing crashed to a halt. "Really?"

I questioned this because I was so surprised. Had we gone this far? Had we been dealing with this for so long that we had written a book that tells us how to die? How much physical pain had inspired this thing? How much anguish creates such a thing? The scale of what was happening seemed to be clearer to me than ever before. This was an ongoing thing, it was not specific to Aids, only pain. It reached deep into the heart, and resounded deeper still to everything that we're about. The meaning of living seemed to turn inside out, yet it never seemed clearer. I simply had to do something to help my friend and it was a part of life, like protecting a baby, or calming someone in distress, or offering your hand to the frail and old who fall in the street. It was basic compassion. Very few could refuse this to anyone.

I went home after spending about two hours with Marcus. I had the idea of looking through my address book to find someone who might know of this book, or even better, might have a copy. I had to be careful who I spoke to about it because, after all, it was a dodgy subject. Many would not be able to understand. They might think it was for me. I didn't know how worried to be about it. When did I start committing a crime, if ever? I thought of asking Gaia about it but rejected this quickly. If I told her at all it would have to be well after the event. Even then I wouldn't give any incriminating details like where and when, although who and why would probably come up time and time again. Eventually after fingering buttons, then changing my mind, picking up the receiver, then going to make a coffee, I thought of someone. He was a writer who had been around since gay began. He had been involved in demonstrations, campaigns, newspapers, and now seemed to have settled on gay fiction. I had once skimmed over an article relating to suicide that he had written. He would know about the book and had probably read it. I had about five different numbers for him but I guessed he would be at his London flat in Covent Garden.

"Hello, it's Paul, from Earl's Court." There was a pause.

"How are you?"

"You don't know who it is do you? I came round to your flat. Gorden from Flex agency sent me round. You said I could call."

"Oh, Paul, sorry of course I remember you, how could I forget?"

"I've got a favour to ask you."

"Well, why don't you pop round and see me. Are you still working for Flex?"

"No, but I'm still working."

"Oh good, well, why don't you come round this after-noon and we can kill two birds with one stone."

"Great! I'll look forward to it." I did find him interesting and he wasn't ugly.

"How about six o clock. I've got dinner at eight. You remember the address?"

"Of course." Everyone knew his address. "See you at six then."

I spent the rest of the day doing nothing in particular apart from shaving, cleaning, doing my hair, making an effort. I always felt as though I was making the best of a bad job when I primped in this way. I arrived at ten to six and had to wait outside his flat until he arrived exactly on time.

"Sorry have you been waiting long? Am I late?"

"No, I'm early." I felt awkward.

We went upstairs.

"So how can I help you?" He gave me his full attention.

"I think maybe we should talk about that afterwards."

"Very good. If you prefer."

We did the business and I noticed how I enjoyed being touched. It seemed like ages since I had had sex with Rick and I hadn't done it for fun since. Sometimes when I was working regularly I would forget to have recreational sex altogether. On a practical level my orgasms would be used up. I think this made me different to other people my age. I didn't have the same drive, to hang round parks, or toilets, or wherever. When I did get round to having sex, it had to be worth it. I expected it to be either very exciting or in some way extreme. I know it's not the same having punter-sex, but it did seem to satiate something. I think I missed what Rick gave me, but there was nothing I could do about this.

Washing the cum off our hands we sat down to have tea and slices of fluffy white bread with home made jam. He seemed to know how to make the whole event nicer. He gave me the money, a figure he had arrived at which was just more than the going rate.

"And you're not to spend that on anything sensible." I

did find him funny, trying to relate to me. "So tell me, what is it that you wanted me to help you with?"

"To cut a long story short, I have a friend who wants to die. I remembered that article you wrote last year. I thought maybe you would know something about a book you can get, about suicide."

There was a pause. Presumably to sort out in his head what I had just said. I expected this. Then he forged out of it with useful information.

"Yes, I do know of a book, although I don't have a copy. What I do have are photocopies from it and various sources that I found interesting. Of course I also have the article I wrote. Now it's very hard for me not to ask questions but I know it's none of my business. If on the other hand you want to talk about it, I would be happy to listen."

"No thanks, not yet, maybe at some point. I would love to read your article. I don't know much about it all really. It's just my friend wants to know."

"Fine, just so you know, you can call me anytime about it."

"That's really nice of you, thanks."

I got photocopies of the copies and went home with my bundle and spent the night under a duvet reading, until I fell asleep. The whole of the next day, I carried on reading. I became an expert in something I wouldn't have guessed at thinking about a few months earlier. Most of the information came from an American book in which they use the term 'self-deliverance' instead of suicide. I found it creepy for the most part, not because of the subject matter, but for the way it was written. Of course the book was intended to be read by a lot of people who for religious, legal, or moral reasons, might find it shocking or ungodly. But there seemed to be a distinct air of manipulation about it. For example, the word 'narcotics' was used to refer to drugs administered in hospital, whereas the same drugs administered at home for assisted death were 'easers of pain and suffering.' I knew Marcus would be interested in talking about this. Marcus had an eye for truth and the distortion of it. He liked nothing better than to root around a subject to find out what was really going on.

103

I gave Marcus the whole bundle and reminded him to be careful as to who sees him reading it. There was a section on social aspects of terminal illness. Another on laws relating to suicide and assisted suicide, and also examples of 'self-deliverance'. The first section was irrelevant because we didn't care what anyone else thought, it was between us. The second was useful only in reminding me that I could get charged with manslaughter. The third seemed like fiction. In each new chapter of this section it conveniently covered different aspects, giving a very one sided view of events. The dialogue seemed contrived. Marcus and I ended up acting out the short scenes. We put on voices: the wife, the doctor, the son, and so on. We tried to recite bits off by heart, making it up where necessary. We laughed so much that one of the nurses came over to comment on it. She said something that was meant to be funny but really meant 'keep the noise down.' We laughed even more at how predictable her comment was. We eventually quietened down feeling good at our understanding of each other. I sat happy at this. I knew he felt the same.

Generally when I visited Marcus I would reel off a list of things I had done or just things I had thought about. He would tell me what was going on in the ward and what he had seen on t.v. When he was tired or lethargic he would say he had done nothing and had nothing to say. These were the times I wasn't very good at, just sitting, spending time with him with nothing going on. Thankfully, he usually had the energy to try and make me feel comfortable, even if it was just a simple gesture like a wink. Sometimes, if he had his eyes closed, he would make a funny face or blow a kiss.

The most useful information in the reference material were the lethal dosages of various drugs. It wasn't as simple as taking loads, because some could make you vomit and then some of the drug would escape. Ways round this were to take travel sickness tablets and have a light snack so that the stomach wasn't empty. There were ways of backing up the overdose like getting into a cold bath, so that hypothermia or even drowning occurred once consciousness was lost. Another back up was to put a plastic bag over the head, making sure it was tight, then to securely tie it around the neck so that it wouldn't come off. In the book they suggested using a ribbon. Why a ribbon?

Marcus decided that he would just IV some smack.

"At least I can enjoy myself on the way. I'd like to go to the very limits and then right off the edge." (This made sense to me.) ". . .And I want you to be with me."

"Ah . . ." This was suddenly different.

"What?"

"I mean sure." Now my fear opposed my reasoning. I guess I shouldn't have been shocked. We were good friends after all. I didn't know if I could actually be there, see it. I hoped I wouldn't let him down. The plan was firstly for him to get out of hospital. Meanwhile I had to get lots of stuff: ecstasy, cocaine and heroin. Then we would have the best drug-fucked party we could and get so high that we wouldn't mind the finale. Marcus would then do the heroin and hopefully I'd still be able to function enough to go home. I would take Rohypnol go to sleep and when I woke up it would all be over. Marcus would be dead. Then I was supposed to go round and let myself into his flat. I would find him and clear up any evidence that showed he'd been with someone else.

The event went beautifully. I bought enough drugs for about five people. Marcus was claiming sickness benefit and hadn't used it whilst he was in hospital, so I cashed all his money up to date and went shopping. I got decorations for his flat. I went to a window display shop and bought lots of funny things. I decided that I would make his whole living room look like a summer picnic. I bought grass reeds, big plastics flowers, a gingham table cloth, tiny details like rubber insects and frogs. I hung huge wads of cotton wool from the ceiling for clouds and a glittering gold ball for a sun. I even bought BBC sound effects of river banks and bird song along with his latest pop favourites. I got cakes and sweets, ice-cream and anything he liked that he could still stomach. I also got marijuana and all the mixes for his favourite cocktails. Between us we created a space that felt right, with nice tastes and things to look at; somewhere which we felt was our world. The other was locked behind the front door. His physical pain was made bearable with morphine. He lay on his settee which was now a grass verge with weeping willow branches hanging overhead.

"I should of had the flat like this long ago," he said.

"It would be hell to clean," I said seriously.

"Nature doesn't need cleaning. It cleans itself."

"This isn't real nature though."

"It's real enough, rather it's as real as I need it now."

"Me too."

I had bought about twenty needles just in case. We started off with the ecstasy. I had made sure that they were ones which made us feel affectionate and loving. We mixed a little coke with it so that we would be chatty. After our first rush we just lay quietly feeling gorgeous, with rosy cheeks, and a smile that stretched right around our heads. It took about a quarter of an hour before I suggested that we snort some more coke to clean us up a bit. This worked perfectly. Soon I was jumping around in front of Marcus making him laugh. He had got his make-up out and was half geisha and half his imagination let go. We knew we had plenty of time ahead of us, so I could help him remove it later. He did joke about being found like that, or with a big smile painted on his face. I had bought rubber noses and ears so these were added to the endless list of looks we thought up. He could be a pig lying with a huge piece of chocolate in his hand, or a dog with a leather harness on, with the CD repeating 'Old Mac Donald had a farm,' because we were high we went on and on. We laughed so much for so long my stomach really ached. Hours passed by so quickly. At one point we checked the clock and fifteen hours had passed. The phone rang every now and then, and his recording played. It said that he had gone away for a few days, so messages were left. We continued, up, down, rushing then not, resting and injecting some more. We cried and laughed as we remembered what we were doing there, until eventually it was time.

"I've changed my mind," he said. "Really I have." Then he burst out laughing. "It's a shame to go when life feels this good."

"But it doesn't usually does it?"

"Yeah, yeah, yeah, I know. I was only kidding."

"What, you mean you haven't got Aids?"

"Not for long."

Again we laughed and laughed at how brutal we could be about something so ugly.

"Okay this is it." We were silent. The CD played a track called 'A whispering wind through chimes'. I helped Marcus with his tourniquet, his arms were so skinny and his veins quite messy by that point. We were really wasted. He put in the needle and kind of frowned a smile, closed his eyes heavily, then opened them again wide. He fell into himself as his life gave in. He held my hands and pulled me towards him. I collapsed on him, squeezing him tight.

"Marcus? Marcus?" As if it needed to be said that I loved him. He knew I was there every second of the way.

I lay with him for a little while then thinking this was morbid I took more coke to get myself together and quickly left. I had planned to go to Josie's for two reasons: so that she would back me up if necessary, and because I thought I might not be able to go through with it all by myself. She had already agreed and said that she wanted to help me. If being there to go to sleep with was the way, then she would willingly help. As I closed the door of the flat, the click of the latch seemed like the switch going off, no more life. By the time I reached Josie's I was a mess. I was crying and could hardly speak. She took control of the situation.

"Now just nod, so I know what's going on. Did he do the smack? Paul, did he?" I nodded.

Josie put her arms around me and sat me down. "Listen Paul I'm going to get you a drink and I want you to take some Valium. Don't worry everything's going to be okay." She went to the kitchen and came back with a vodka. "Drink this, there's two Valium here. I want you to take these to relax. I don't want you to go to sleep. It's best if you calm down first. You've been very brave." I began to

107

cry more ferociously than before and could hardly breath. "Don't worry, Paul, I'm here, Everything's going to be alright. I wouldn't lie to you would I? Would I? No, see now take these."

I swallowed down the Valium and kept on drinking the vodka. I began to retch then held it back.

"Come on Paul, look at me." She pulled my face around to look at her. "Look at me. Everything's fine."

I saw her face and I was distracted and started to quieten down. She pulled me down to lie on her lap and stroked my head.

"You're so kind Josie."

"Nonsense, it's just part of what I'm here for. I want to do this."

I remember being confused by what she meant by this, but had so much else on my mind it just joined the confusion. It was early evening but Josie closed the curtains anyway and put a candle on for light. I began to melt into a softer more manageable state.

"Josie, I'm so scared that I will not be able to deal with this. I might be haunted by this."

"Don't be stupid, this is what he wanted and you proved to him how much you loved him."

"It's just so confusing. I've been told all my life that this is bad . . . you know . . . that life is sacred."

"What is more important in life than love?"

I needed to hear that so much. Slowly out of the manic turmoil came twinges of good feelings, which seemed to merge around thoughts of Josie and Marcus. After a couple of hours I was given some sleeping tablets, and slept.

I woke into a soft haze. I got in the bath and had a shave. The Valium wasn't enough to stop my anxiety rising. I started to feel guilty about the drugs I'd taken. I had been trying to stay clean. I didn't really want to do them. I justified it by thinking that it was a one off and it showed that I didn't have a real problem anymore. I lay lifeless, the bath water cooling. Surely I should feel more guilty about what I'd done to Marcus, rather for Marcus. I didn't know which got to me the most. I knew I felt disgusted but I had no sense of perspective. I wondered what Gaia might say. I tried to reason but felt only surges of emotion.

"I did it for Marcus," was one of the voices in my head.

"What? Killed him?" was another.

I was hard on myself that day, but this was common. Usually it had more to do with drug come-downs than anything real. The trouble was though it always felt real so it still had an effect it definitely still hurt. It got deep so that it scratched and even scarred the foundations from which I tried to work.

With these feelings and a jumble of others, Josie and I caught a cab round to Marcus's and let ourselves in. As could be expected the flat did not look like how I thought I had left it. Josie held my hand as we entered the mess. Sitting in the middle of the storm-struck room was Marcus covered in sick, snoring but definitely breathing deeply and soundly.

"I don't believe it, the bastard's not dead!" I said as I dropped down beside him.

"Jesus Christ!"

After shaking Marcus, he came to. We worked it out that he must have been sick and passed out because he obviously wasn't dead.

Things were suddenly very different. Did we have to go through all that again? How much more confusing could life get? I felt like dismissing the whole thing and just going away somewhere, away from London, from Aids, and emotion, like there was such a place in this world.

Josie made some tea and we sat chatting, avoiding the most obvious question. Did he still want to die? Marcus told Josie about what we got up to and it was nice for me to see them together. I had a tendency in life to keep friends separate. Since I had stopped the drugs, it felt easier to see one person at a time. On a one-to-one there seemed to me a more positive attitude of helping each other. As soon as more people were involved, strange things began. This had to do with insecurities, egos, competition and personality clashes. I was still being affected by the Valium and not quite sure of the impact that this situation was having on me. My friend was to be dead and he wasn't. Should I be happy or sad? How soon should we try again if he still wanted to and if he didn't had I made the right decision to begin with? I sat watching the two of them but my mind was all over the place. I was certainly relieved that I didn't have to deal with officials of any kind. Could I go through with it again? In the bath earlier I had decided that I could never do it again. This was actually the same thing though, I just hadn't done it yet. I said no in my head but I was coming down off drugs. As usual I was scared, and the decisions I made weren't necessarily coming from my depths.

"How do you feel Marcus?" I squeezed in when there was a break.

"Shaky, sick, funny?"

"I bet," Josie said.

"Well, Marcus it's Thursday morning, Christmas is two weeks away. It's the beginning of your second life. How are you going to live it this time?"

Marcus looked like he was going to say something so Josie and I were ready to listen. After a short while nothing had come out. I looked at Josie and she looked at me. As we turned back his eyes were wet. It seemed as though I had lost the plot again. What could be going on in his mind? Some people lived their whole lives without ever having to face up to anything more than a change of clothes and Marcus sat deciding, life or death. To my eyes he became a boy, injured and lost. It became clear to me what my role was now.

"Marcus, I don't want you to do it again. Of course I want what you want and I can see there's no good argument against it, but I have to go against reason, and you . . . I just don't think I was made to be able to do this . . . I don't want to help you die. Marcus I want you to live as long as possible. I might be being selfish. I might be a complete coward but I think this is what I really want. Marcus I don't want you to die. I want you to stop hurting but not like this . . . please! If I could change what's happening, somehow, god knows how, I would, but not like this."

110

I couldn't look up but spoke into my lap. I didn't know where the words came from but I think it was somewhere which was really me, somewhere far inside and wasn't governed by what anyone thought, right or wrong.

Marcus got hold of my chin and lifted it. He knelt up. "I'm sorry Paul."

"It's not for you to say sorry, it's just all so grim."

Marcus seemed to be smiling through his tears. "I don't know if I want to die either, but I know what I think of you."

His expression engulfed me and I was instantly happy. "Look at you, surrounded by grass and flowers, your Highness, king of the fairies."

Josie began to laugh. "The place does look great." Now there was silence and beaming faces. "More tea anyone?" she continued putting on an old woman's voice.

I got up. "Yes please granny. Listen to this track. It's called 'A whispering wind through chimes.'"

I sat back down behind Marcus with him in between my legs and rubbed his shoulders.

"God that feels good, Paul."

It was decided that Marcus would put everything on hold for a while and see how things went. We cleaned up the flat and spent Christmas together on our fantasy river bank.

Marcus died on the tenth of January. He had been in a coma and let go one morning while I was asleep. Although I had been saying good-bye to him for sometime, it was no more easy when it came. There's no point in thinking how unfair, why so soon? all that stuff. That was just how it was, what we all had to get used to.

CHAPTER EIGHTEEN

I was adamant in not going to Marcus's funeral after how I had felt at Kevin's. Josie told me that she wanted to go, saying: 'He was one of those people who had always been there, and I thought always would.' She reminded me the service was meant to be part of a healing process. A time and a place to say good-bye properly. What if I regretted not having gone? This seemed a pathetic way of dealing with anything in life, but I went just in case.

Rick arranged to pick me up after the service. It was good to see him. He didn't bring his new boyfriend. I had spent so much time with Marcus over the last few months I had neglected seeing Rick. It was probably for the best. It gave him necessary space. This was obviously what he wanted. He seemed happier. Now that I had more time for him again, he had less time for me. I wasn't his 'number one' anymore. I had to decide if what he had to offer me with the boyfriend was enough for me. I did expect a lot from my friends so couldn't make this decision straight away. I thought that I would let time give me the answer.

Again the funeral was only useful in serving as a focus for my anger. I asked if I could say something during the service. It seemed to me that maybe others hadn't known how good Marcus was. It wasn't the most obvious thing about him. I sat alone in my living room listening to songs that reminded me of him. Not knowing where to start, I wrote a list of his qualities. Then I thought if someone hadn't seen these things in him it would seem abstract. I didn't want that. I looked at photographs of him. I tried to explain in what way I liked him but this seemed idiosyncratic and self-centred. Maybe something romantic to help people cry. This might come across as being pretentious. It wasn't that I minded people thinking this of me, I just didn't want it to detract from what was meant to be going on. Maybe I didn't know what was really going on.

I felt like saying: 'This is all a bag of shit, this fucking disease, and every sad feeling that has ever been caused by it.'

This would be too disrespectful to his parents, who had made time to come all that way on that very special day. I loved him and he was so beautiful to me, but did I just want to hear myself say this? Why should I want to share that with people I didn't care about. Did I simply want them to know how I felt? Had this all been removed from Marcus the instant he died? He wasn't going to be there. He didn't care who said what, or even if anyone turned up at all. This was now just about my feelings and their feelings.

I decided not to speak at the service and saw it as a failing. I also decided never to go to another funeral and hoped I would never need to. Josie was with me all the way, which helped. Everything seemed easier with someone to talk it through with. I had thought before then that I didn't think unless I spoke, but that definitely wasn't the case with emotions. I felt them whether I spoke about them or not, although it seemed as though I didn't deal with them unless I spoke.

I had met Marcus over seven years before. I was in London for the weekend, having travelled up from Brighton for fun and adventure. Seven years, that's a quarter of my life. What was the point of making new friends? How much longer did I have? How would my illness and eventual death affect the people around me? It's odd living your life knowing the outcome. Of course everyone knows they will die but naturally they are given a lifetime to prepare for it.

I just had to carry on, to go to the gym, to meditate, see my therapist, to think of other things to do. I decided to do more prostitution, save up some money and take a holiday. This was a harsh thing to distract myself with, but I needed such a distraction. Working hard takes up a lot of mental energy. I joined an agency in the West End which had a reputation for being the best. I had a haircut, took a course of sunbeds, made myself look as presentable as possible, and went in for the interview.

"Do you suck?" the man said sitting in an office which hadn't been decorated since the Seventies. It looked and smelt like everything had an inch of nicotine coating it.

"No"

"Not even with a condom?"

"No." This wasn't for safety, I just found it too degrading. My interviewer obviously disapproved.

"That's fine, we need to get these things sorted out now. You don't mind getting sucked?"

"No . . . I mean no I don't mind getting sucked."

"Do you get fucked?"

"No, I'm a top." I thought I'd better say something encouraging here before he gave up on me altogether.

"So you fuck?"

"That's right." I knew it didn't sound too good, but I also knew I looked okay, and I was acting very friendly.

"Do you kiss?"

"No."

"Have you done this kind of work before?"

"Yes, about five years ago. I did it one summer to pay off my overdraft." I wanted him to think I had experience but was still a fresh face. I had to fill out an application form stating what hobbies I had, what countries I had visited. This was meant to show what kind of company I would be if escorting. I knew it was nonsense and most of the customers wanted sex, but I went along with his silly charade. I think it was also meant to make me think the agency was special or glamorous. I just hoped that he didn't believe it.

I had to get a bleeper, which I wore on the inside of my trousers, not that I minded people thinking I was a prostitute. I did mind them thinking that I thought I looked like a doctor on call, and they knew better. When working I had to be ready for action at all times. They liked to have their boys available as much as possible. I got plenty of work, the bleeper seemed to go off whenever I sat down to eat, or bath, or spend time with friends. I could have 'signed off' whenever I wanted, but these things take up all of life so I would have never been able to work.

I saved money quickly for I didn't have a wish to spend it. I didn't go out at night time and hardly felt like shopping, I just wasn't up to it. At least work seemed to have a purpose. It meant I didn't have to think about getting sex, which can take up all of every day, with the bonus being that I got lots of money.

I saw Josie at Lighthouse as usual. Although I was still going to therapy I was letting it take a back seat in my life. I had tried so hard to sort things out, to make things work, thinking that Gaia might have the answers, yet all we ever seemed to do was discover more questions. I know she helped me deal with Marcus. As a counsellor she was able to respond well to my grieving, but when we dug all that came up was shit. I was prepared to keep at it though, assuming I was unaware of what was happening within me and that Gaia presumably knew the plot.

I got a telephone call one night from a punter. From the conversation we had I knew he was going to be difficult. With agency work it's hard to turn someone down just because I didn't like the sound of them for the agency would lose the money as well. I took a cab. When working at any of the more famous or chic hotels, it was best not to arrive on foot. I was inspected by the receptionists. I was well used to this and sometimes even asked them if there was a problem. They could only guess what I was there for, even though I felt like I looked and walked and talked like a whore, but they had to put up with it. I knew that at worst all they would do is phone up to the room to check if their guest was expecting me. The agency demanded that I wore a suit when going to the hotels but I never bothered. I could hardly be expected to dress like that all the time just in case I got bleeped.

The customer was German and looked like every other German customer I've ever had. All customers from the same country seem to look alike. He was tall, fair, sun-tanned and very clean looking. I recognised his attitude as a punter.

"Maybe we can do it again and again, maybe all night."

I could tell that he thought it was completely up to him, that I had no say in what happened. "Maybe you might enjoy it too." He was what I expected, over confident and forceful, if not aggressive. I was a toy, his sex toy. He wanted to get fucked. I had to tie some string around my balls so that the blood would stay in my dick to keep it hard. If

115

someone couldn't get a hard on with me, I would hate them to use string to keep it hard. I would think they weren't turned on to me. He didn't mind. I think it was more about an object being up his arse. It was something he wanted and could have. He could even have it hard if he wanted it. I think these things were more important than the sensation, or at least more of a turn on. Whenever I say to Gaia maybe it was this or that or this, she always says maybe it was all of them. I really don't know what was going on in his mind. It could have been none of them. Who knows? It may have been a way of relieving tension and sharing his wealth.

I fucked him once. Then he ordered some food. To me this didn't make things any nicer, it just seemed to reiterate: 'This is really civilised and you will enjoy this if I tell you to.' I ate and talked just to kill time. I knew that if he wanted to get fucked again then he would have to pay double. This punter told me all about his family, about his beautiful house, how marvellous his life was. I thought to myself, how many other people in your life simply put up with you for some other reason? It seemed hard to believe that he had one personality which he kept for people he liked, and one for me or other prostitutes. Hopefully I experienced the facade and the 'other him' was the real him. Maybe he was really lovely, and it was I who had brought with me into the situation the abuse, the disrespect, and hatred. Maybe it was both.

He did want to get fucked again and argued when I told him about the price. He even phoned the agency to check that I wasn't lying. They backed me up and he was willing to pay, but not without a struggle. Then he even asked could we work something out between ourselves. As though after all this I would still want to collude with him. I explained that I could get into trouble with the agency if I did. When I worked at Flex I agreed to a deal like this with another punter, then he turned around and said that he would tell if I tried to charge him. I did charge him and got the sack. So with the German I said no, I didn't trust him at all. After all the haggling, the phoning, the checking, quite happy to

116

get me into trouble, he said okay. Again he suggested that I would probably enjoy fucking him. By this time I hated him so much that I had to go to the bathroom and just sit and calm down. I thought to myself: 'I could just leave. I could tell the agency that he was messing me around and wouldn't decide and because he had already phoned they would probably believe this.'

"No just do it, get it over with."

"But I can't."

"Yes you can. Be strong."

I had mentioned to Gaia before that I could handle most things in my life when I felt strong. She had said that what I meant was: When I could put up a strong enough barrier. This was very different from dealing with things from a position of strength.

There was knocking on the door.

"You're not going to spend all night in there are you?"

"Shut up you mad bastard, I hate you." I screamed inside my head.

I faked a laugh.

"No, I'll just be a second."

"We don't want to waste anymore time do we? Come along."

He must be insane, I thought. How can two people interacting be getting it so completely different. This seemed scary. How often in life does this happen? It could make me lose faith in communication altogether. "Come along," he called knocking continually on the door.

I pushed open the door violently knowing he was behind it. I caught his toe quite badly.

"Oh I'm so sorry, I didn't realise you were still right outside."

He hopped around the room like a cartoon character whose foot has been hit by a mallet. How I wished I had a mallet. How pathetic was I, that I had to stoop to banging someone's toe with a door and pretending it was an accident. "I'm so sorry, what can I do to help?"

The punter calmed down in time to get fucked again, crouching on all fours, with his face to one side flattened

117

onto the bed. He reminded me of a wounded animal with it's front legs broken. His moans though seemed to have nothing to do with pain, but more his notion of what someone getting fucked was meant to sound like. There was a mirror to one side of me at head and shoulder height. I could see myself moving back and forward but the bottom half of me and the punter was cut off. I smiled to myself, then really smiled surprised to see myself there smiling. Then I rolled my eyes as I thought about what I was doing there. I knew he couldn't see me, so started to make faces. All the time he continued his groan. "Aah, Aah, Aah. Fuck me, Aah."

I made a face like a squirrel and even brought my hands up to mimic eating a nut, but they smelled of condoms and arse so I stopped. I carried on with this slow repetitive action until my dick got too sore from being tied up so long. "You're going to have to cum." I said.

"Oh I was just getting relaxed." I wouldn't be surprised if he had been daydreaming and forgotten I was there. I had been doing everything within my power to do the same, which I'm sure is an odd thing for the mind to have to deal with, receiving a physical sensation and trying to think of other things which are completely unrelated.

"I can't carry on much longer." I tried to make it sound as though this was because it was so pleasurable and I was about to cum.

"But we have twenty minutes left."

I obviously had no choice.

"I'm going to cum . . . oh, ah, I'm coming." I knew I was no good at faking it, but did my best.

"No, no, not yet."

"Sorry it's too late."

When I took my dick out he checked the condom to see if there was any cum in it. Luckily there was some pre-cum and lubricant.

"You don't cum much, do you?"

"No not the second time, but it feels just as good." I pretended that this was the issue.

"What about me?" he said, putting on a grotesque face

which was meant to be like a sulky little boy.

I jerked him off, although he protested that it wasn't enough. I knew the agency would expect no more of me. I got my money and left, again having to argue about what the agreed figure was.

When I got home I was completely exhausted. I felt like I had been kicked around and shat on. The smell of rubber wouldn't wash of my hands. On the way home I bought some chocolate as a treat. I sat and began to eat it, then thought this unhealthy, so stopped.

I wondered how different this punter was from ones I had done when I was high. Maybe the difference was simply that I wasn't high. It seemed that I wanted to protect myself more from the German, but in fact I think I had to build a stronger wall to do this, so maybe I actually damaged myself more. I certainly tortured myself by staying when I wanted to leave. At least on drugs I didn't care to leave, so maybe that was less hard on myself. The drugs could be seen as another wall. Maybe this drug-wall was a false protection, leaving me susceptible not being able to tell if I was being affected or not.

I looked down at my fingers. They were brown, the chocolate had melted as I daydreamed. Now they smelt of chocolate and rubber. Again I thought, I deserve to eat this, and again fought against this and threw it in the bin. At least I wouldn't have to think about it again. I did lick my fingers, it seemed somehow that I had already okayed eating this much.

I enjoyed doing nothing, and wondered if this was how I should be spending my time. It seemed like a relief after putting up with such a hideous punter. I knew I couldn't compare my whole life to this. It's not a very high standard to gauge from. I should be making the most of my time, making every minute count. How many years had already past since my diagnosis? It goes so quickly. The funny thing was that most people tended to live life faster, faced with this. How could I slow it down? I could read, but if it's interesting, time races by. If I did something boring or tedious my time would drag by. I could get up early and watch my clock, counting each hour of the day as it goes by. It would be excruciating, but it would be slow.

I decided at this point that I wanted to go out. I wanted to take some drugs and have sex in the way I used to. I reminded myself that I was creating my life and I had to have confidence in what I chose to do. I have been guided by my mother, by Gaia, by all my friends but I must remember that what I am is partly due to what I have chosen to be. I had to think what I wanted to do, how I wanted to spend my life. Marcus had tasted this and he enjoyed his freedom, I think, even at the expense of losing his family and people who could not understand him. Leaving them behind as he lived. Marcus knew he had less time than most. I knew for me there was always a struggle between wanting to live life to the full and just wanting to live. Gaia said that she thought that I had given up drugs to protect my health. This upset me. The idea that I might like myself, might want to protect myself, maybe even respect myself enough to care.

I went into the West End alone, caught the end of the bars and then went on to a club. I took some ecstasy and danced like I hadn't danced in years. The music was mine, it had my life in it, my memories and all my dreams. There were people in the club that I hadn't seen since last I was there. Some even seemed to be standing in the same places, but I didn't care. I was there for myself to get what I could out of it. I talked with people I didn't know. I laughed and drank and someone asked if I had seen Marcus. I told them that he had died and secretly smiled at the thought of the twisted fun we used to have. I felt as though I understood what it was all about, the dying, the drugs, the sex, and everything else you feel like you understand when you're high. I danced some more and thought of what I was, and what I had wanted to be, about lovers I had never had, and of friends that gave me more than I could ever have wished for.

I looked down from a balcony over the crowds. How could I dislike any of these people, anyone of them could have been Marcus and probably are to someone else.

The feelings of love and acceptance seemed as real as any I had ever had. In fact they seemed more real because at least I knew that the drug was having a physical effect on my body. It was real, whereas usually there was always room for doubt.

I recovered slowly over the next week and continued with more passion towards my goal of going away. I bought my plane ticket two weeks in advance and tried to save up my money. I did as many punters as I could possibly stand, and as usual just a few more.

CHAPTER NINETEEN

I was tempted to go to New York but opted instead for sunshine and Miami. There had been moments during the flight when I stepped outside myself, saying: 'What do you think you're doing? Who do you think you are?' To which I was still too unsure to answer. When I was taking lots of drugs I had thought that I was in the last phase of my life. But sitting on the plane I felt as though I had options. Of course they were still within the framework of dying but how and how soon might be more up to me. Now that I was taking more care of myself things that had been wrong with me and that I had attributed to HIV seemed to have gone away. It was clear that my ill health had more to do with my lifestyle at the time. It was the lack of hope that had often made me cry, and the horrible thought that this was all I deserved. Why I thought, should I expect anything else, anything better?

I lounged in a café bar on Ocean drive close to my hotel. Every cliché about sun and sand washed through my senses, but not over them. I wasn't going to let this slip by like a life misspent. I devoured the offerings as the junky within me cried: 'Feel that! Oh and that! And that! And that!' Collecting these treasures and burying them deep within me. I could expect to need these memories at anytime.

"Ah, that feels nice. Give me more, yes, how special."

An ugly goblin tore these things out of the space around me and used them within to nourish. It had been a long time since I fed so well. I was starving.

Having been there a week I finally began to relax. Whilst sitting on the beach I gently itched my feet on the sand. From the blue of the sky and the sea came a young man. He sat down next to me. I wanted to say excuse me I'm busy, but quickly saw how this seedling could also be good to eat, to be swallowed whole in fact.

I was wrong.

I had been so self-absorbed. I had run along the beach early every morning before the crowds and heat. I had swam in the sea, jumped and splashed making my body use itself for what it's for, for living. So often, even though I exercised at the gym, I felt as though it was all just facade. I'm not athletic and would see myself doing a jigsaw puzzle rather than anything sporty. I think I was wrong to say this to myself, and to do this to myself. Over the past week I had fallen asleep, as the setting sun made my skin glow with a warmth that I would expect to have to buy or earn somehow, not just be given as though it was mine to have. I had sat and meditated as the crashing waves allowed me to ignore them, but not in a bitchy way, but with a kindness of allowing themselves to just be a part of what was around me. They didn't want to bug me or make me want to shout 'fuck off!'. This place had been very nice to me, like a nurse who always has the right kind of smile and makes you wonder if it could possibly be real.

I had been so self-absorbed that I had neglected to see what was happening to me. I felt great. This seedling had sat down next to me, because to him, all that could be seen was a stranger, fit and calm, someone I didn't think I was. It was an illusion, like everything I appeared to be. To others, what I called an illusion, came across as what I really was. This seedling was, I realised as he spoke, in fact a seed. I, who had only ever been shit, felt comfortable talking to this man, and he seemed to not want to let go. Somehow we talked about me, and my illness, and my drug problems, and anything else that revolved round me, but the strangest thing was that we were actually talking about him. Although my 'me' talk sounded tied to my ears, he grasped at it with desperation. I couldn't refuse or resist him, I wasn't sure which.

This young man's name was Scot, and I couldn't shake him off. I was alone so it was one of the last things in the world I wanted to do. Scot was scared and HIV positive and young. I wanted to take care of him, that's for certain. I wasn't certain up to this point that I would ever be capable, but it just happened that this was what came out of me and headed straight for him, the seed.

The light seemed staged by something clever and show-off, the breeze effective and loving. The sounds were not harsh but comforting, assuring that I was a part of this something whole. The smells made me hungry, my responses this simple, yet so complex that it couldn't be contrived. Scot was my company, who I couldn't have chosen, not before he sat with me. We let ourselves be wrapped by everything around us. This was not a selfish thing, no matter how I tried to make it so. Everyone was allowed these treats. They had always been there just waiting for me to accept them. I knew too well a life without them and so did the seed. It changed for me when he sat down. Scot didn't point anything out to me but as we spoke I felt a welcoming deep within. I had a realisation of what I was doing, as though I had been shaken kindly and someone said,

'Look at what you are.'

'What am I?' I would have had to say.

'You're fine, that's what you are. You're something you wanted to be.'

I could have pretended not to know what this meant, but that would have been the me who wouldn't admit that things can change, telling me that I couldn't be what I wanted. That me was getting told to hush, instead of shouting down anything that tried to have a voice, no matter how sweet it might be to hear. This voice was rising and it was so different for me to have inside my head. I'm not saying that it was sure beyond all else, but it was strong enough to hold onto, and wonderful enough to not allow it to peter out. So it sang and it was given lessons by the things that happened around it, the things that gave it a purpose and made it useful. Along with it, all of me was fed these things, and it made me feel like I was growing.

Dear Josie,

I am enjoying every second of this place. As you can see from the picture it's idyllic.

Love Paul.

124

I bought some plain postcards that had no picture on the front, just a square for the stamp. I found this funny. On Josie's I drew the most basic seascape, not child-like but simple and without any passion. I also sent one to Loz. I didn't draw on it but wrote.

Dear Loz,

I think I'm changing. I think it's a good thing. I love you.

Paul.

I spent the rest of my time in South Beach with Scot, 'hanging out' as he called it. We didn't have sex, I don't think it would have been what I wanted, but I didn't have a choice. I know that he was very confused and that sex was a focus point for some of the pain relating to his status. We met in the mornings for breakfast, we walked together, he showed me round, we worked out together, but when evening came he went home and I went back to my hotel. I spent a lot of time with my windows wide open, reading, thinking or simply breathing the fresh sea air. When I left for my flight home, Scot drove me to the airport and we kissed and hugged good-bye.

"You're welcome to come and stay, anytime," I said.

We both seemed sad to leave each other. He held my hand as I checked in, and squeezed it harder than I think he was aware of. His face scrunched and he shifted around uncomfortably as I said good-bye.

"We will keep in contact won't we?" he said as though to reassure himself.

"Sure," I said completely unsure that either one of us would still be alive in a year.

On the plane I wondered that if we weren't both positive, would we have come together in the same way? I felt we wouldn't have. I wondered how many other people on that plane were considering when their life might end. At this point this became something I couldn't forget. Whenever I

125

was in a crowd, in Queer street, or at the gym, I thought to myself, how many of these people know their status, are aware of their T.4. cell count and are monitoring it's rise and fall? How many of these people count their KS sores or any of their symptoms on each new development? In every situation my answer was: Too many. What a strange thing to have at a party, or a club, or any fun gathering of friends. Nobody invited it but it came all the same. What was our weapon against it? Was it advanced science, or government funding, or public sympathy? No, it was something that comes from the sick, the dying, and those around them who really care. It was the attempt to understand what was really going on.

CHAPTER TWENTY

I got back to London and, yes, I did feel stronger. I found that I could be alone more easily and enjoyed just letting the day go by. I tried not to waste my time but sometimes just sitting and staring into space felt good, as long I made myself aware that I was doing it because I chose to, not because I couldn't be bothered to do anything else. So like the cliché of the old people on the park bench, I sat and thought about things that had happened in my life. I tried to kindle warmth from the good times and see the bad times as just part of what got me this far. It is only in retrospect that I could see it like this. No, I didn't think that it answered the questions of the universe of why and how? But it helped me accept the shit. Why accept the shit in life? I don't know. Maybe because there's no point in not, it's there all the same.

It was only two months later that I started to get ill. I could no longer work for I had shingles across my abdomen and back. I had to go onto sickness benefits. A social worker helped me sort it all out, which was necessary. I would have just sat and waited to die by that point. I knew it was going to be a continual snowballing of things going wrong, and I could have given in there and then, but my social worker was very kind. He made things easier for me and I think for everyone around me. Josie liked him. She even thought he was cute. Yeah, so what? Who needs a cute social worker? There again why not? I thought, how ironic it was that one of the kindest men I had ever met got paid to be nice to me. God, how often I had faked a smile for money, or an orgasm for an Arab, and so many other things to myself? There I was being shown faked concern. Of course, some would say that he really did care, and that it was what he had chosen to do, and it was good that he got paid to do something he really cared about. I was just so aware of how important this was to me and it was this that was sad. I was bothered whether my social worker cared. I needed him to care. I needed a man to touch me when I felt so ugly, so scared, and not quite resigned to the situation I was in. To show me that there were people left when all the facade was gone, all the charm, all the strength, all the sparkle from my eyes, and all the sex I had ever used to get the things I wanted. Josie cared. Loz cared, she travelled every other day to see me in the hospital. She put her own life on hold.

"You've been injured. I want to make sure you're alright."

As always Loz's words rang through my mind. She had said *alright*, not well. It's not my body that's been injured, it is simply weak. Loz knew my other wounds. I began connecting things I had disconnected, making me feel like I had a heart that knew my soul and it had played a part in my life. I hadn't been a shell who got it all wrong, who had made one mistake after another with no idea of plot, or depth, or other people's feelings. What a power to have, what a strength to give. I saw this in Loz the first time we spoke in that little café in Brighton. I had seen how she could touch the very life of me, hold it and keep it safe in her heart.

"Loz this is Josie."

My mouth was swollen and dry, but I couldn't help grinning, seeing them both together at the corner of my bed.

"Josie this is Loz."

On the twenty-second of May, I died at the age of twenty-nine, just three months after I arrived back from Miami and five months after Marcus had died and only two weeks before the death of James who got my bed five days after me.

Like so many, I had just wanted to be able to do as I chose. After all, modern medicine had arrogantly held the hand of God since long before I was born. All was curable, or would be one day. Yet I got sick from having sex. How old fashioned, how barbaric, how absurd. And there are weapons which can do the most ludicrous things like pinpoint and destroy from the other side of the planet and I died from having sex.

What had I found worth living for? I can count how many

times over my life that I thought: How lucky am I? Once in Morocco at the age of twenty, during the college summer break. I was on a scooter riding through the countryside on a road scratched out of the mountain and heading for a place called Paradise. I was with a beautiful friend, and we laughed and laughed and laughed just because we were happy. I could feel air pockets whizzing by, refreshingly cool then reassuringly warm. I shouted to my friend as I drove up beside him, our T-shirts flapping in the air. "How lucky are we?" And he looked at me and we laughed again.

The next was when I drove through Malibu with a cowboy in a pick up truck, well as real a cowboy as I was ever going to bother finding. The sun burnt my arm which rested on the open window. The hillsides were brown from a summer of parching. It was so simple, the man gave me pleasure, no upset or lies or making me feel like I wasn't enough. The only demand he made was to be allowed to enjoy giving me this.

The last was in an ocean, splashing and squawking during an escape from London, a holiday from a brothel I worked at when I was twenty-one. I was by myself. I felt free and independent. I hadn't a care in the world that could penetrate such bliss.

There were not many of these times for me and none of them was when I was working. None of these times was when I was high, no matter what combination of special drugs I took, no matter how fabulous a party I was meant to be at. None of these times was when I had released myself from everything constructed. Bound in ecstasy beyond all my sexual desires. These weren't the times that were special.

I know that it takes all sorts of times to make a life but when I was a child I wanted so much more. I saw men on the television, I looked at men in my mum's catalogues and they seemed different, they were what I wanted, not pain, anguish and Aids. I had spent my whole life it seemed for men, by men, at men, and I thought that they were worth dying for, or maybe it was the freedom I thought was worth dying for.

129

My happiness didn't come from succeeding, getting to where my ambitions directed. No it was the times when I felt the sun, the air, the water, the things around me that give life. This was when I was truly happy, this was when I cared whether I lived or died. I was so stupid, I went back to the prostitution, I went back to the men who I dealt with so badly, to a cloudy sky, to a life I had created that went against my childhood dreams. Should I have let my fantasies be real?

Who will care that I am gone? A wonderful Josie who wipes her tears on my sheets, being comforted by Loz with whom I never understood exactly what we had, but I knew it was good. A mother who arrived too late and who cared too much in the wrong kind of way, who'll be left with the greatest pain, that of never having really known her child. She sits and stares and says to herself through her confusion,

"Who are these women?"

"Where are the men?" There'll be lots of questions that she will ask, then make up the answers herself.

Before my death I couldn't see her often, not carrying all that pain. It was too late to explain, and if I wasn't sick it would always have been too early. This was cruel of me and cruel of her. Mine was out of resignation, hers was out of fear. I had hoped that she would get some comfort from a certain letter. And Loz did start it so many times for over two years, until finally she decided that she wasn't able. At least the idea had given me some peace of mind. My mum was to come to terms with my death in her own way. Loz was not her God, neither her forgiver, and not even her teacher now. It was too late.

Gaia came to see me the day before I died. This had upset me more than I expected. I think she was the mum I tried so hard to sort things out with, the mum who could understand, who could listen to my graphic stories and want to help me feel good about my life. After following the guidelines on grief in her textbooks, she will work it all out. I think she did care.

These women are at my bedside. I never would have guessed that this would be the case. This would be what the end of my life would be like. There was no sex involved with any of these women and I thought that sex was so much in life. I remember thinking it affected everything I did but I guess that world of mine wasn't the whole of my world.

I hadn't even told Rick I was in hospital. The last time I saw him, his glowing face told me all I needed to know about his life and the love he'd found. I couldn't be a part of that, so I decided to stay away.

My sheets were taken and washed, my bed made up again, my pillows, 'the' pillows, fluffed and readied for another day, another death. My flowers that Josie had chosen were thrown into the garbage. Everything that showed I was there, I had lived, was taken away. I didn't need the mysticism of a funeral but I did want it to be easiest on everyone concerned. Whether they burned or buried me it's only the physical me that goes. Then there's nothing left apart from 'their' memories and 'their' feelings. The very things that make up a soul.

Photos will help keep their memories fresh for a while. Until the photos become the memories, like those from childhood, indistinguishable from the photos that proved them. Finally even these are gone along with all the people who felt their feelings and then I am truly dead.

If I could live my life again, would I have been a prostitute? Would I have taken the drugs I did? Would I have had the sex I had? My answer to all of these questions is no, but that's only if I was able to keep everything I've learnt from them. Otherwise I would go through everything again.

Also Available

Packing It In
David Rees

This collection of essays, written and arranged to form a year long diary, opens with an all too brief visit to Australia, continues with a tour of New Zealand and a final visit to a much loved San Francisco, before returning to familiar Europe (Barcelona, Belgium Rome) and new perspectives on the recently liberated Eastern Bloc countries (highly individual observations of Moscow, St Petersburg, Odessa and Kiev). Written from the distinctive and idiosyncratic point of view of a singular gay man, this is a book filled with acute and sometimes acerbic views, written with a style that is at once easily conversational and utterly compelling.

'Rees achieves what should be the first aim of any travel writer, to make you regret you haven't seen what he has seen . . .'
                                                                    Gay Times

ISBN 1-873741-07-3
£6.99

A Cat in the Tulips
David Evans

Both in the later flush of life, Ned Cresswell and Norman Rhodes, room-mates of pensionable age, set off on their annual weekend visit to enjoy a traditional spring break in a quiet Sussex village. Where angels would fear to tread, in rushes the feisty Ned – whilst the conciliatory Norman becomes more reluctantly involved. The village begins to hum, including various brushes with the law, an exciting cliff rescue, a hard-fought game of Scrabble, Agatha Christie in Eastbourne and a dreaded Sunday sherry party, the weekend lurches socially from near disaster to neocataclysm. Further complications ensue, despite Ned's forceful objections, when the currently catless Norman falls in love with an irresistible pussy looking for a new home. Comedy and thrills combine in this delightful and most British of novels.

'It's like Ovaltine with gin in it.'
Tony Warren, creator or Coronation Street

ISBN 1-873741-10-3
£7.50

Heroes Are Hard to Find
Sebastian Beaumont

A compelling, sometimes comic, sometimes almost unbearably moving novel about sexual infatuation, infidelity and deceit. It is also about disability, death and the joy of living.

'Highly recommended. . .'   *Brighton Evening Argus*

'I cheered, felt proud and cried aloud (yes, real tears not stifled sobs) as the plot and the people became real to me . . .'
                                        All Points North

ISBN 1-873741-08-1
£7.50

The Learning of Paul O'Neill
Graeme Woolaston

The Learning of Paul O'Neill follows the eponymous hero over nearly thirty years – from adolescence in Scotland in the mid-sixties to life in a South Coast seaside resort in the seventies and eighties and a return to a vibrant Glasgow in the early nineties. As the novel begins, fifteen-year-old Paul is learning fast about sexuality as his Scottish village childhood disintegrates around him. After many years in England, he returns to Scotland trying to come to terms with the sudden death of his lover. His return brings him face-to-face with the continuing effects of adolescent experiences he thought he had put behind him. And his involvement with an ambiguous, handsome married but bisexual man raises new questions about the shape of Paul's life as he arrives at the threshold of middle-age. This is an adult novel about gay experience and aspects of sexuality which some may find shocking but which are written about with an honesty that is as refreshing as it is frank.

ISBN 1-873741-12-X
£7.50

On the Edge
Sebastian Beaumont

An auspicious debut novel which combines elements of a thriller and passionate ambisextrous romance and provides an immensely readable narrative about late adolescence, sexuality and creativity.

'Mr Beaumont writes with assurance and perception. . .'   Tom
Wakefield, Gay Times

ISBN 1-873741-00-6
£6.99

Millivres Books can be ordered from any bookshop in the UK and from specialist bookshops overseas. If you prefer to order by mail, please send the full retail price and 80p (UK) or £2 (overseas) per title for postage and packing to:

Dept MBKS
Millivres Floor
Ground Floor
Worldwide House
116-134 Bayham Street
London NW1 0BA

A comprehensive catalogue is available on request.